Prisoner Within

Jenny Ford

Prisoner Within 3rd Edition

Published By:
The Endless Bookcase
Suite 14, STANTA Business Centre, 3 Soothouse Spring,
St Albans, Hertfordshire, UK, AL3 6PF
www.theendlessbookcase.com

Print On Demand Edition:
Also available in multiple e-book formats.

ISBN: 978-1-914151-45-3

Acknowledgement

Writing this book, and bringing it all together, would have been a hard task without the help from my amazing publishing team at The Endless Bookcase.

I am extremely grateful to the lovely Morgana Evans, the always patient publication's manager, for her continued support and always being there when I need valuable advice.

I would like to extend my sincere thanks to Rebecca Adams - Life, Business & Mindset Mastery Mentor for her much valued endorsement. I very much appreciate it.

I also wish to express my thanks to, Claire Harris - Book Talk Radio Club for writing the foreword.

I would love to know your thoughts and comments about this book

You can leave your feedback via the retailer you purchased from or on my website.

Thanking you with gratitude.

Jenny xxx

www.jennyfordauthor.com

https://jennyscourse.thinkific.com/

https://www.jennyfordauthor.com/product-page/write-to-release-journal-pen

About the Author

Jenny Ford, an award-winning and multi-genre author has a narrative style that takes the reader on a journey through the eyes, ears and emotions of the main character of each book. Jenny inspires and empowers her readers by impacting their lives; making a difference with the written words in her books.

A very successful beauty therapist with her own business, Jenny's life and career was turned upside down when she was diagnosed with Multiple Sclerosis. Jenny had no idea that she would end up becoming an author and says, "No one was more surprised than me when I wrote my first book. I had no interest in writing at all, not even as a child. I literally just fell into it and it has now become my passion. I guess you could say I was Divinely Guided!"

The main focus of Jenny's writing is positivity - she loves writing stories that make people smile and says, "I am continually inspired and gain motivation by the different people that I meet every day, which drives me to be the best that I can."

Jenny goes on to say, "I am a strong believer that everything happens for a reason and truly believe that without the knocks and challenges, I certainly wouldn't be where I am today!"

Foreword

I've known Jenny Ford now for just one year and have grown to appreciate not just what a great writer she is but also a very wonderful and compassionate loving human being! Her generosity of spirit and genuine love and care for others shines through in her story-telling. Prisoner Within is a great example of Jenny's beautiful writing; nominated for a Prestigious Global Award by the Author Elite Awards in 2018, the book has just been revised and edited and I am honoured to have been asked by Jenny to write a foreword.

Prisoner Within tells a powerfully moving story which follows the main character Amy on her journey of heartache and pain leaving her with nightmares that she is unable to let go of. Can she forgive the one person who caused this and find the inner peace and freedom that she is so desperately searching for? Losing the people that she cared for the most leaves Amy living in a foster home. Feeling scared and alone Amy struggles to settle into her new surroundings. How will she cope with living with strangers? Will Amy ever be happy again? Becoming a prisoner within her own mind Amy finds it difficult to let anyone in pushing away those that care for her except for Tara. Tara is Amy's best friend and rock, over the years she has seen Amy go through the highs and lows and wants to help her friend get through the nightmares so that she can be free to live a life of peace and happiness.

In these times of Covid, so many of us have lost someone dear to us or know someone who has…..will the pain ever go away? Will we become 'Prisoner's Within'? There is hope and there is light at the end of the tunnel and Jenny Ford's story telling in this wonderfully written and compassionate book is sure to offer hope.

Claire Harris – Book Talk Radio Club

https://www.booktalkradio.info/

Prologue

The house was dark, and it had gone quiet. Amy lifted the covers from over her head, slowly got out of bed and walked towards the door. Nervously turning the door handle, a shiver went down her spine. Inch by inch, Amy opened the door, drew in a deep breath, and continued. She had a feeling that something was very wrong. Step by step, Amy made her way down the stairs. She stopped for a moment before stepping onto the last step. When Amy entered through the kitchen door, she felt something sharp under her foot. Amy bent down to see what it was; a fragment of glass had cut her. Amy wiped away the blood with her hand, and feeling scared, she walked further into the kitchen. Amy gasped as she put her hands to her mouth, unable to scream. She stood there for a moment in a complete daze before she picked up the phone and called the police.

Chapter 1

"Amy, Amy, wake up sleepy head you will be late for school."

"Mum, it is too early, just five more minutes."

"Amy, get up now!" scolded Mum.

Amy dragged herself out of bed and went down into the kitchen. Josh, Amy's older brother, was sitting at the table eating his breakfast. "Morning squirt, you're looking tired, didn't you sleep well?"

"No, Mum and Dad's arguing kept me awake. Will this ever end Josh?" sighed Amy.

"Amy, if I have to work several jobs to save enough money and get you and Mum away from him, then that is what I will do. I promise," Josh responded, with a serious look in his eye.

Amy adored Josh. He was her best friend, and she looked up to her big brother. She always felt safe knowing Josh was around to look out for her. Dad was an alcoholic and a gambling man. Mum was the loveliest person, trying to keep everything together. There would always be tension in the house when Dad was home. On rare occasions, there were days when it would be peaceful and calm, but those days were few and far apart.

"Amy, have some breakfast." Mum put a bowl of cereal on the table.

"I'm not hungry," Amy replied grumpily.

"Amy, you must eat before school, it is the most important meal of the day. You need to keep your strength up!" Josh smiled at Amy.

After breakfast, Amy went to her room to get ready. Josh left for work. Dad had already gone.

Amy enjoyed being at secondary school. She was very creative and loved it. Her art teacher was always complementing Amy on her work. "Amy, you are so natural when it comes to sketching, and you use colour very well." Amy liked it when her teachers praised her work. This was a happy place for Amy to be, but unfortunately, the stress of her home life was always on her mind.

That evening after dinner, Dad came home drunk… and in a foul mood. He had been gambling again and, by all accounts, had lost a lot of money. Mum would get really cross with him, as they were tight with money as it was.

"Why do you do this all the time? We do not have enough money. How am I supposed to pay the bills and put food on the table?"

"Shut it, woman!" he would shout. "Just go and get my dinner!"

"Get it yourself!" Mum would shout back at him.

Well, that was it; again, the arguing started. Dad called Mum lots of nasty names and sometimes even hit her. Josh and Amy would take themselves to their rooms to avoid hearing it all. It was horrible and made Amy feel so frightened for Mum. Amy got on with her homework, and as soon as things had quietened down, she fell asleep.

***

"Morning everyone," came this quiet voice, as Dad walked into the room.

"Morning, Dad," said Amy and Josh.

"Children, go and get your coats," Mum would say.

"What is the rush? It would be good to sit and talk to my children occasionally," snarled Dad.

"Amy, Josh, go and wait outside. I will be there in a minute," said mum sharply. She then turned her attention to Dad. "Talk with your children? I am surprised if you can make sense of anything after the state you always come home in. You ought to be ashamed of yourself, letting the children see you like that all the time."

Dad walked out, muttering under his breath.

This is what Dad did every time Mum mentioned his behaviour. He would walk out as if nothing had happened.

***

It was a few days away until Amy's Thirteenth birthday. Mum wanted to do something special for her.

"Amy, how would you like to invite a few of your friends over for your birthday? A small party?" asked Mum.

Amy laughed. "Mum, you call them gatherings, not parties."

Mum chuckled in response.

"Do you think that it is a good idea though? You know what Dad can be like…" Amy asked.

"You leave your father to me. I will have a word with him." Mum gave Amy a nervous smile.

***

It was the weekend and Amy's birthday had arrived. Things had been a bit more peaceful at home since Dad's last outburst.

"Happy birthday Amy!" Mum and Josh pulled out some party poppers and sang a lovely birthday song to her.

"So, squirt, you are now officially a teenager. How does it feel?" Josh teased Amy.

"I shall let you know later. It has only been a few hours, Josh." Amy smiled.

"What time are your friends coming to your gathering?" Mum chuckled.

"Around six o'clock, it will only be for a few hours. It makes me nervous about Dad being here," said Amy anxiously.

"Dad will not be back," Mum reassured Amy. "Now go on, it is time to open the presents."

Josh gave Amy a small box wrapped in pink paper. Amy unwrapped the paper excitedly and opened the box. Inside was a stunning bracelet. Josh had a message engraved on it: *Happy birthday Amy, love you.*

"Oh, Josh, it is amazing. I love you too. Thank you." Amy gave Josh a big hug.

"Your turn Mum," said Josh. Mum also gave Amy a small box wrapped in purple paper.

"I wonder what this is?" smiled Amy.

Amy unwrapped the paper and opened the box. "Mum, it is gorgeous!" It was a lovely sparkling necklace with the words: *The most precious daughter a mother can have.* Amy looked at Mum and started to cry.

"Why are you crying?" asked Mum.

"Because this is the best birthday ever."

Mum held Amy in her arms and stroked her hair.

"Dry those tears, and go and do something with Josh, so I can start on the food," said Mum, as she walked back into the kitchen.

Amy and Josh went to Amy's room, laughing along the way. Mum smiled and wiped a tear from her cheek. She had not seen Amy this happy in a long time.

"Who is coming to this gathering of yours?" Josh asked Amy.

"There are four girls in my class at school."

"What are their names?"

"Polly, Alice, Michelle, and Sandra. Will you be staying with us Josh?"

"I am going to see Toby, but I will come to the end of it," Josh promised.

"Josh, I am worried about Dad, in case he turns up whilst my friends are still here. I don't want him to spoil it for me," said Amy worriedly.

"Hopefully he will stay away. You just concentrate on having a good time, you are only thirteen once," exclaimed Josh.

Mum laid the table with all the food, and Josh put the music on. As Amy came into the kitchen, Mum and Josh gasped in surprise. Amy looked so stunning wearing a blue and red dress, matching shoes and the bracelet and necklace that mum and Josh gave to her. "Amy, you look like a princess!" Mum smiled with pride.

"Thank you, Mum," Amy beamed.

Amy's friends soon arrived bringing cards and gifts for her. "Thank you everyone, I will open them later."

As the night went on, Amy and her friends were having a really good time singing, dancing, and catching up on all the latest school gossip.

There had not been that much fun and laughter in the house for a long time.

The gathering continued longer than expected. They were all having so much fun messing around. By this time, Josh had returned home from seeing Todd, just in time to light the birthday cake. Mum lit a number thirteen candle, and they all sang happy birthday to Amy at the top of their voices. Amy smiled from ear to ear. "Open your presents Amy," one of the girls urged. In excitement, Amy ripped the paper off. Amy was delighted with her gift of a new journal and pen, a pink and grey top, a pair of fluffy slippers, some sketching pencils and a book.

"Thank you all so very much, I love them!" Amy exclaimed.

Mum and Josh watched Amy enjoying herself. "Amy seems to be having a good time," Josh noted.

"Just relaxing for a while without any dramas feels refreshing," Mum said.

"It will be just the three of us one day Mum, in our own little house," Josh promised.

"You are a good boy, Josh," said Mum, with a loving expression.

"There is one thing I do not understand though. Why have you stayed with Dad for so long? He has behaved so badly towards us."

"Josh, it is hard to try and put into words. I have always hoped that your father would change his ways, but over the years, his drinking and gambling have just gotten worse and that is when all the arguments started. I just keep hoping things will change," exclaimed Mum.

"So, why stay? It has been horrible, not just for you, but for us too."

"I'm not sure," said Mum sadly. "Maybe I still love him."

"But Mum, he hits you, and there are no excuses for that," Josh said with a dark expression on his face.

"Please try to understand Josh, that someday, you and Amy will leave. I do not want to be on my own…"

"But Mum, you will not be on your own. I will always take care of you, and so will Amy," Josh said exhaustedly.

Just then, the kitchen door flew open. Dad had arrived home, drunk. Thankfully, Amy's gathering was coming to an end.

"Amy, your friend's parents are waiting outside to take them home," Mum said nervously.

"Thank you for coming, and for my amazing presents. It has been a lovely birthday," Amy smiled.

"Wherr' has everyone gone? The party has jusss' started…" slurred Dad. "Come dance with me!" he said as he grabbed Mum by the arm. She shrugged away from him. "I said ddance with me!" Dad shouted, starting to get irritated by Mums lack of enthusiasm.

Josh took Amy upstairs, knowing there would be an argument.

"You just had to, today on Amy's thirteenth birthday. This is a special day for her, and you turn up drunk, when I asked you specifically not to!" Mum said, as her blood started to boil.

"Do not go on at me woman, I have only had a couple of drinks."

"It's your daughter's birthday! Show some respect," Mum said, raising her voice even louder.

"I am not drrrunk!" Dad retorted, unsteadily reaching for a can of beer from his bag.

"Oh no you do NOT!" Mum said as she snatched the beer from him. Just then, his fist came up and punched her in the face, splitting her lip as a trickle of blood started dripping down her chin.

"Leave before I call the police!" screamed Mum. Dad left the room, laughing on his way out.

Mum stood there crying. Amy and Josh ran downstairs to the

kitchen, to check Mum was okay. "Are you alright, Mum?" Josh asked, passing her a cloth.

"I am fine, my darling," said Mum, as she tried to smile. "I am so sorry that Dad spoiled your special day Amy."

Amy held on to her Mum tightly. "It will be OK Mum; we'll look after you."

***

From that day on, things just got worse. Dad's drinking and gambling were getting uncontrollable, but Mum still lived in the hope that things would change. They never did.

Josh worked hard so that he could build up enough funds to pay for a small, rented house for the three of them to live in.

Amy dreamt of the day until they could leave and take Mum away to be safe and free from Dad.

***

It was a cold winter evening and Mum had just finished cooking dinner. They were all gathered around the table, when Dad rolled in, drunk as usual and in a worse mood than normal. He announced that he had lost his job. By all accounts, he had been drinking at work.

"What are we supposed to do now?" Mum shouted. "How can you do this to our family? We have lost everything because of your drinking and gambling!"

Amy and Josh quickly got up from the kitchen table and left to go to their rooms. Dad had never been this angry before, and it scared them.

"Why do you think I do it?" Dad shouted back. "So I can drown out the sound of your moaning voice! That's why!"

"There you go, not facing up to your addictions, and blaming everyone else. And now look at what has happened," Mum cried, pacing around the room anxiously.

Amy and Josh could hear the arguing from their rooms. Josh went to be with Amy so that he could try to reassure her that it was all going to be okay. The next thing, all they could hear was Mum's screams. "Josh, please help Mum!" cried Amy.

"Wait here Amy," Josh replied hurriedly, as he ran downstairs.

The screams continued and Amy hid under the covers to drown them out.

When Josh got into the kitchen, he was horrified to see the blood and cuts all over Mum's face, and broken glass spread around the kitchen floor. It was an awful sight. Anger started to rise in Josh, as he looked at Mums distraught state. Dad had hit Mum in the past, but nothing as bad as this. He was going to kill her if he didn't do something.

"I am going to get help Mum. I'm calling the police."

"Go back to your room unless you want the same, my boy," Dad snarled, with an evil look in his eye. He was so drunk and blinded by anger, he was acting purely off of impulse.

Dad was about to give Mum another punch to the face, but Josh ran at him screaming, "Leave her alone! Get off my Mum!"

"I told you to go boy!" Dad screamed, and pushed him as hard as he could across the room. As Josh landed, his head caught on something sharp. Blood started pouring from his head, and he fell unconscious.

"Josh!" screamed Mum. "What have you done to my baby?"

The anger and panic Mum felt was unlike any she had ever known. Mum picked up a knife from the kitchen side and went for

Dad. There was a big struggle, and in the chaos the knife plunged into Dad's chest. He lunged forward at her and collapsed. Mum attempted to move out of the way as he landed on top of her, but as they tumbled backwards, she fell onto a large piece of broken glass that went straight through her. Mum died instantly. Dad was already dead.

***

Shocked and scared, Amy waited for the police to arrive. When all went quiet, she ran downstairs to find both her parents dead on the floor. The sight of all the blood made Amy feel sick. She heard a slight wincing noise coming from the corner of the kitchen. "Josh...?"

As she bent down to him, Amy saw the blood pouring from his head. Amy picked up a cloth and tried to soak up the blood, but there was far too much. "Hang on Josh, help is on the way." Josh slightly opened his eyes, looked at Amy, whispered *Sorry*, then passed away in her arms.

After a while, the police arrived. There were flashing lights and the sound of sirens everywhere... People going in and out of the house taking photos. Was this real, or was it just an awful nightmare that she would soon wake up from?

Chapter 2

Amy was now scared and all alone. It was explained to her that as she had no other family she had to be placed into foster care. Amy just felt numb... *How can this be happening to her? Is this real? Is her brother really dead?*

Gathering together a suitcase of essentials and her most precious items before leaving the house, she went into Josh's bedroom. Looking around, it seemed so empty now, and tears started streaming down her face. Amy decided to take the money Josh had been saving that was hidden in a box in his wardrobe, putting it safely into her case. She knew he would have wanted her to have it.

When it was finally time to leave the house, Amy walked out with tears in her eyes. Unable to look back, she got into the waiting car and it drove off, leaving her family home and her old life behind her.

***

Amy arrived at the foster home feeling very scared and alone. *What will happen to her now? Will she still be able to go to the same school?* She tried not to think about what she'd just witnessed, and tried to forget about the awful events that had happened.

The social worker took Amy inside the house to meet with her new guardians.

"Amy, this is where you will be living now, with Mr and Mrs Robins. They'll take good care of you," the social worker explained.

"Hello dear," said Mrs Robins. "Let me show you to your room." Amy's room was big and bright with lots of butterflies on the wall. "I'll leave you to settle in."

Amy sat on the bed and looked around the room, not really taking it all in. She lay down and cried and cried until she eventually fell asleep.

***

By the time Amy woke up it was the morning. She had a bad feeling in the pit of her stomach, but her memory of the night before was hazy, like a nightmare that she couldn't quite place. *Where am I, what am I doing here?* she thought. She got up from the bed and walked downstairs.

"Morning Amy," said Mrs Robins. "How are you feeling?"

"Why am I here?" Amy demanded, feeling stressed and confused.

"You came to us last night."

"But where is Josh and Mum?" asked Amy. A panic rising in her.

Mrs Robins slowly went over a summary of the details of the night before, reminding Amy of what had happened. Feeling devastated, it all came flooding back, and Amy broke down in tears.

"Oh, Amy," said Mrs Robins, as she gave her a hug. "It will be okay, dear; we will look after you."

***

The months and years passed quickly, and Amy settled into her new home. Children came and went, but Amy just seemed to stay. It had not been easy to start with. Amy was not very keen on her foster parents at first, but they had taken good care of her.

It was difficult for Amy to let people get close to her. Putting a barrier up around herself as protection made her feel safe, and she was not going to allow anyone in; that was until Tara came along.

Amy and Tara attended the same school and became best friends, spending all their time together. Tara was very outgoing, she was loud and hilarious, which made Amy laugh.

Amy had only ever had that closeness with Josh. The memories of that night were still very much with her, and she found she couldn't move on.

It was coming up to Amy's birthday.

"What are we going to do for your special day?" asked Tara.

"It's not a special birthday, Tara. I really don't want any fuss," replied Amy.

"Nonsense, every birthday is a special birthday! How about a party?"

"My foster parents would never allow that to happen," Amy replied.

"But they don't need to know!" said Tara. "Just leave it all to me."

***

It was the day of Amy's birthday.

It was Amy's fifteenth birthday. She never wanted to celebrate the day, not since the traumatic events that occurred not long after her thirteen birthday.

"Happy birthday!" said Amy's foster parents. They handed her a card with £20 inside. "Buy yourself something good."

"Thank you," she said politely. Amy went and put the money away, adding it to the money Josh had saved.

Tara came to get Amy. "Are you ready?" she asked.

"For what?" Amy responded dubiously.

"I have arranged a small gathering for tonight!"

"Tara, you know my feelings about this."

"You will love it," replied Tara excitedly.

I doubt that, thought Amy.

Tara took Amy to an old warehouse that was never used. There were about fifteen of their friends there. They were more acquaintances though really.

"Happy birthday Amy!" they all shouted out. Amy gave a slight smile and thanked them.

One of the boys that was attending the gathering was called Luke. She had never really spoken to him before, but she thought he was rather good looking. He seemed to be in a carefree mood and was obviously planning to make the most of the party.

"Happy birthday," he said to Amy. "Would you like a drink?" he asked as he produced a bottle of cider.

"No, thank you," Amy refused politely, remembering all the trouble alcohol had caused her in her life so far.

"Go on, just one! It's your birthday after all," pressured Luke, in the hopes he could convince her to lighten up a bit. "Just one little sip even?" he badgered.

Something just snapped in Amy. "I said NO!" she shouted angrily and stormed off, heading towards the door. Tara came running over to her.

"What's wrong, are you okay?" asked Tara worriedly.

"You know my feelings about alcohol! Anyway, why does he drink it for? We are only fifteen!" Amy said incredulously. "I am going home now, Tara. Please thank everyone for me. I will see you tomorrow."

With that, the party ended early.

***

The following day, Tara called to see if Amy was okay.

"I am fine, Tara. It's just when Luke offered me that drink, all the memories of that night came back — not that they will ever go away," said Amy. "It just upset me. I really miss Mum and Josh."

"I am sorry Amy; I did not know about the alcohol Luke brought with him."

"It isn't your fault, Tara. Thank you for trying to make my day special." Amy smiled.

"Let us go into town and do some window browsing. We might not be able to buy, but there is nothing stopping us from looking!" Tara suggested.

They both laughed, and headed off to town.

After looking in many shop windows, they happened to bump into Luke.

"Hi, Tara, Amy. How are you both?"

"Good thanks, Luke," said Tara. "How are you?"

"I am fine, thanks. Amy, I just want to apologise for yesterday."

"I am sorry too. I should not have shouted at you Luke."

"Well, can I make it up to you? Would you like to come to the cinema with me sometime?"

"Maybe," Amy blushed. She had never been on a date before.

"Great, I will give you a call. See you both later," Luke replied as he walked off.

The girls just looked at each other and started to laugh.

"You have to go," smiled Tara.

"I will think about it," Amy said seriously.

"What is there to think about? Luke is gorgeous!"

"I have never been on my own with a boy before, Tara, except with Josh..." said Amy sadly.

"Listen, Amy, you have to start taking that barrier down at some point. Why not make the first move and go out with Luke? You may even enjoy yourself."

***

After a few days, Luke called Amy.

"Hi Amy, how are you?"

"I am good, thank you. How are you?"

"Very well, thanks."

There was an awkward silence.

"Would you like to go to the cinema with me tomorrow?" asked Luke.

"Yes, that would be good," Amy responded awkwardly.

"Cool, I will pick you up at five o'clock."

"Bye, see you tomorrow." Amy put the phone down. Her face was feeling hot. She called Tara immediately.

"Tara, Luke just called me. I said yes to going to the cinema with him!"

"Amy, that is really good news... How are you feeling?"

"Nervous. It was awkward, with a lot of silent moments. Luke is coming to pick me up at five o'clock tomorrow."

"There is nothing to be nervous about Amy. Just go and have a good time. What are you doing now? Do you want to come to the park for a while?"

"I would love to, but I have homework to do. I will call you tomorrow," replied Amy as she said her goodbyes and hung up.

Amy sat for a while, thinking about Mum and Josh, wondering what Josh would say about Amy going on a date. Amy smiled and got down to doing her homework.

***

The next day Luke picked Amy up at five o'clock.

"Make sure you have Amy back home by nine young man," her foster mother said.

"I will, Mrs Robins," replied Luke.

Luke decided to make a night of it and took Amy to get something to eat before going to the cinema. Amy was having a great time and was pleased she'd agreed to go along.

"What a weird film. I have not laughed that much in a long time," Amy chuckled. "It was hilarious."

They took a slow walk back, laughing all the way. Luke got Amy home right on time.

"Thank you so much, Luke. I had a really lovely evening," Amy gushed.

"Can I see you again soon?"

"I would like that," smiled Amy, feeling a flutter in her stomach.

Luke gave Amy a little peck on the cheek and left. Amy touched her tingling face and smiled as she watched him walk away.

***

After that night Amy and Luke went on many more dates and became very close. But Amy was still not ready to tell him about her past.

19

School term was coming to an end for Amy, Tara and Luke, and it was time to start looking for a job.

They drifted in and out of work, not really finding one that made them happy.

Out of the blue, Tara announced that she had got a job on a cruise ship, singing.

"Tara, why did you not tell me?"

"I thought I just did?" Tara laughed.

"You are such a comedian," chuckled Amy, "I knew you could sing, but I did not think you wanted to do it full time."

"Neither did I, but there is not much else I am good at, so I thought I would give it a try. What are you going to do?"

"There is a job vacancy for a secretary at a solicitor's office; I thought I might apply for it. Luke has decided to go to college. He wants to do carpentry."

"I thought that was something he didn't want to do?"

Amy explained, "If Luke could at least learn a skill, then he would always be in work!"

"That makes sense, and a wise decision," smiled Tara.

"Look at us, all grown up."

"Well, some of us are!"

Amy and Tara laughed so much they were crying!

These were the choices they had made, and that is what they did.

Chapter 3

Amy got the secretarial job in a solicitor's office and Luke became a qualified carpenter, whilst Tara was living her life as a singer on a cruise ship. Amy would talk to Tara as often as she could.

"I miss you so much, Tara."

"I miss you too Amy."

"How are things at the solicitors? What is it called again?"

"Higgins and Cromwell. Really, Tara, you have a head like a sieve!"

"You know me!" Tara laughed.

"It is going really well and keeps me busy. I work with good people. How is the singing going?" Amy asked.

"It is the best job ever but very tiring."

"It must be so exhausting for you, Tara, standing there singing away enjoying yourself!" teased Amy.

"Actually, it is. There is no need for sarcasm." Amy could not stop laughing. "How are things with Luke?"

"Fine," said Amy.

"That doesn't sound very convincing!"

"Honestly, everything is fine. I am going to see him later. He wants to ask me something."

"Sounds intriguing. Tell me all about it when I come home in a few days. I must go now, Amy. I will see you soon. Love you."

"Love you too," said Amy.

Amy wondered what Luke was going to ask her. They have been together for a long time now, and she enjoyed his company.

Luke arrived with a bunch of flowers for Amy. "Thank you," she said as she kissed him on the cheek. "What are these for, it is not my birthday?"

"Does it have to be your birthday to buy you flowers?" Luke joked.

"No. They are lovely," replied Amy.

"But there is something I wanted to ask you Amy."

Amy looked at Luke and could see he was a bit nervous. "Are you okay?" Amy asked.

"Amy. We have been together for a while and I think we should take our relationship a bit further."

"What do you mean a bit further?" Amy was feeling nervous now.

"We should find our own place and live together?"

Amy went silent, not expecting that. She was starting to feel slightly panicked about the idea of taking this huge step forward.

"Luke, I am happy as we are."

"So am I Amy, but I want us to have more time together…"

"Luke, we do not need to live together to spend more time with each other. I am not ready for that sort of commitment just yet. We are both still young."

"But, Amy, I love you," pleaded Luke.

"I know you do Luke. And I love you, but living together, I am not ready for that. Just stay the way we are, at least for now."

Luke was not very happy about Amy's decision, but he reluctantly agreed.

***

Tara was due home from her cruise. Amy was really looking forward to seeing her. She did miss their girlie chats.

Amy was preparing a welcome home meal for Tara. Luke popped by to see if there was anything Amy needed.

"Thank you, Luke, but I have everything now."

"Have a good time. Say hi to Tara for me. I will call you tomorrow." He gave Amy a kiss on the cheek and left.

"Is anyone home?" Tara suddenly asked.

"Tara!" Amy ran to the door...

"Mrs R let me in." They gave each other a big hug.

"You look awesome with your golden tan. Must be all that sea air."

"I feel amazing. Absolutely glowing," smiled Tara.

"Take your bags upstairs. I will put the kettle on, and you can tell me all your news."

Amy and Tara made themselves comfortable on the sofa.

"I have missed you so much Tara. Tell me, what is it like sailing around the world? You must have met lots of fascinating people?"

"Amy, you would love it. It is hard work, but the benefits you get from it are amazing! I get to go to the most wonderful countries, not that I get too much time to sight see. I eat lots of different types of food and of course, there is all that glorious sunshine!"

"It must be a bit of a shock then, coming back to rainy old

England!"

They both laughed.

"Tell me. How is it all going with you and the job?"

"I am really good and so is work – I love it there. A lot of paperwork to do, but I am enjoying it."

"And how is everyone? Are there any new arrivals?"

"My parents are fine," smiled Amy. "We had a few foster children come to stay temporarily, but they have gone to their new adopted families now, so it is just me."

"And how is Luke?"

Amy went a bit quiet.

"He is okay."

"Come on," said Tara, "spill the beans. What has been going on with you two?"

"Luke wants us to find a home and live together," Amy burst out.

"What is wrong with that? You have been together long enough."

"But I do not want to live with him."

"Amy," Tara paused, "do you love Luke?"

"Yes," replied Amy.

"So, what is stopping you?"

"Tara, Luke is a wonderful man. He is sweet, kind, and gentle... but I just cannot make that commitment to him or any man."

"Amy, Luke would never hurt you. You really have got to let go of this fear of yours."

"I try so hard Tara."

"Amy, you have to tell Luke. He deserves to know the truth."

"When I am ready. All I want to do at the moment is spend time with my best friend," Amy smiled.

The next six weeks flew by. Amy and Tara had so much fun being out with their friends, going on shopping sprees. And Tara being her normal flirtatious self!

"I hate it when you leave," said Amy.

"I know, but it will not be forever."

"It sure feels like it to me."

"Promise me you will tell Luke everything?"

"I will try," replied Amy.

***

Amy was enjoying her job as a secretary at Higgins and Cromwell.

"Morning everyone."

"Morning Amy," came the reply from her colleagues.

"Amy, can you get me a coffee please?" asked her boss Mr Higgins. "I want to have a talk with you."

Amy's face blushed. *What have I done?* she thought.

Amy knocked on Mr Higgins door. "Come in Amy, sit down." Amy put the coffee on his desk and sat down.

"How do you like working here?"

"I am enjoying it very much," Amy replied nervously.

"Good, I am happy to hear that. My Personal Assistant, Dawn, is leaving the firm, and I am looking for someone to take her place."

"Gill is awesome at her job," Amy suggested.

"Amy, I am not asking you to suggest someone. I am offering you the position."

"Oh." Amy sat in silence while Mr Higgins continued.

"Your duties as my Legal Personal Assistant will be preparing correspondence and legal documents. Reviewing and proofreading outgoing documents to ensure they are error free and that they comply with legal procedures. And to occasionally accompany me to court. There will be a big increase in your pay, and you will receive private health insurance."

Amy was shocked. "Mr Higgins, I am very honoured that you have asked me, but there are people that have been here a lot longer than me with more experience."

"Yes, there are Amy. I see a lot of potential in you and your work. You have ambition and drive. You are very efficient and organised. I like that about you. I need to fill this position quickly. Dawn leaves in two weeks' time. What do you think?"

"Yes, of course," smiled Amy. "I would like that very much Mr Higgins. Thank you."

Amy could not wait to share the news with her foster parents and Luke. She thought of how proud they would be when they found out.

But when she arrived home, there was an ambulance outside. Amy's heart dropped as she rushed into the house, imagining the worst.

"What's happened?" Amy asked.

Tears streaming down her face, Amy's foster mother explained, "It is your dad. He had a heart attack and died a few minutes ago."

Amy could not believe it. She had lost her whole family once already; this could not be happening again so soon! "But Dad was fine this morning. How could he have a heart attack?" Amy asked desperately.

"He was not in the best of health due to him being diabetic, and overweight. I guess his heart could not take it," Mum explained. Amy held mum in her arms and wept quietly. Amy's good news did not seem important anymore, as once again tragedy surrounded her.

***

On the morning of the funeral, Amy helped Mum to get ready. "What am I going to do without him, Amy?" she asked, distraught.

"You still have me mum, and lots of support from all the children that you and Dad have fostered over the years," Amy offered, in an attempt to look at the bright side. Mum gave Amy a slight squeeze of her hand and left the room.

Tara looked at Amy standing alone with a sad look on her face. "Are you OK?" Tara asked.

"Not really," Amy replied. "Today has brought back memories of my parents and Josh's funeral. And now I have to say goodbye to my foster dad too."

"Just remember that Luke and I are here for you Amy. Whenever you need us," Tara replied, not knowing what else she could say.

Amy accompanied her Mum to the waiting car. There was a long line of past foster children, now grown adults, standing outside to support the lady that gave them a start towards a better life, and to honour the man who was always by her side.

Chapter 4

It was the first day of Amy's new job as Legal Personal Assistant to her boss, Mr Higgins. Amy was extremely tired after another sleepless evening of nightmares. Feeling nervous, Amy walked into the office. Her colleagues were a little disappointed that none of them were offered the job Amy was given, but they were happy for her all the same.

Amy made a coffee and went straight to Mr Higgins office to get her instructions for the day.

"Morning Amy, are you OK? You look a little tired."

"I am fine," Amy smiled meekly.

"How is your mother doing?"

"It has been a difficult few weeks, but she is OK, thank you for asking."

After Amy's meeting with Mr Higgins, she went about her day.

Higgins and Cromwell were solicitors in corporate law advising businesses on their legal obligations, rights and responsibilities. Nigel Higgins and Matthew Cromwell were partners as solicitors. They had a good reputation and were respected throughout the industry.

Amy's first day as Legal Personal Assistant was exhausting. All she wanted to do was have a long soak in the bath and an early night. She got into the warm bubble bath, closed her eyes, and relaxed.

The following evening, Amy was preparing dinner as Luke was coming over. "Mum, I have some news to tell you. My boss promoted me to his Legal Personal Assistant."

"Amy that is wonderful news. I am so proud of you. You work very hard, you deserve it," Mum smiled.

"Thank you, Mum."

Just then the doorbell rang. "I will answer that," Mum replied. "Hello Luke."

"Hi Mrs Robins."

"Amy is in the Kitchen."

"How are you?" Luke hugged Amy.

"I am fine, sit down, dinner is ready. How was your day?" Amy asked Luke.

"Good. I have just finished building a set of drawers for a customer and it will be ready for delivery tomorrow. How was your day?"

"Busy. I forgot to tell you, I've had a promotion at work."

"That is amazing. As what?" asked Luke.

"I am now the Legal Personal Assistant to my boss, Mr Higgins."

"When did this happen?"

"A few weeks ago. It was the day Dad died, and then we had the funeral… I've not found the right time to tell you."

"Congratulations, does that mean we can now start looking for a home of our own to live in?" Luke asked hopefully.

Amy started to feel very irritated, "Luke, are you joking? I made it perfectly clear to you before, that I am not moving in with you! We said we would leave it for now."

"But that was a long time ago. Amy, it will never happen, will it?"

Amy looked at him. "I am sorry Luke."

Luke got up from the table and left. Amy felt saddened but at the same time relieved. She cleared away the dinner plates and went to bed.

It was not long into her sleep that the nightmares began again. Amy woke up suddenly, sweat dripping from her head. She cradled herself and sobbed. *Will this ever end?* she thought.

***

It was several days since Luke walked out on Amy. She had not heard from him at all during that time. *Was this the end of their relationship?* she wondered.

Amy was glad that it was the weekend. After a relaxing Saturday morning Amy decided to go into town and do some shopping. Walking around the shops for a few hours, Amy's feet were beginning to ache. She found a small coffee shop, ordered herself some herbal tea and took a much needed sit down to rest her feet.

Whilst looking through her bags, Amy heard a voice. "Hi Amy." Amy looked up and standing there was Luke. "May I sit down?" Amy nodded. "How have you been?"

"Just fine Luke." Amy said sharply. "You walked out on me. I have not heard from you in ages and now you ask me how I am?"

"Amy, I needed time to think about us, our relationship. Amy, we keep going around in circles and ending up at the same place. Nothing is moving forward."

"I do not want to live with you. Is that the reason for all of this?" Amy said, feeling angry.

"No, well, partly. We have been slowly drifting apart from each other for a while. You will not let me get close to you, and when I do you switch off. I love you very much Amy, but I cannot carry on like this. I feel it is best that we end the relationship."

Amy looked at Luke with tears in her eyes. "I agree. I am truly sorry that I have hurt you Luke. For what it is worth, I do love you too, but I know I can't commit any more than I already have."

Luke gently touched Amy's hand and left. Amy wiped a tear that was trickling down her cheek. "Goodbye, Luke," she whispered.

***

Amy focused all her attention on her job now that she was no longer with Luke and was extremely busy anyway.

After work one evening, a few of Amy's colleagues went out to the pub.

"Amy, would you like to come for a drink?" asked Gill.

"No, thank you," Amy politely replied.

"Amy, how long have you been here? You have never been out with us. It will be fun."

Amy felt a bit awkward as she always refused. She really did not enjoy going to pubs.

"That will be lovely. Thank you," she replied.

They went to a small pub just around the corner from work, called Harry's Bar.

"What would you like to drink, Amy?" asked Gill.

Gill was secretary to Matthew Cromwell at the solicitors and was always kind to Amy. "Just an orange juice, please," said Amy.

"Would you like something a bit stronger?"

"No thank you, I do not drink."

Amy was enjoying herself. It was good getting to know her work colleagues outside of the office.

"Amy, I am so glad you came," said Gill, as she passed her the orange juice. "If I did not drink, it would save me a lot of money," Gill laughed. "How are you settling in as Mr Higgins new Legal Personal Assistant?"

"It is a lot more work, but I am enjoying it."

"You landed on your feet getting that role." Gill smiled.

"I do feel guilty. You and some others have been there longer than me," Amy said uncomfortably.

"Amy, Mr Higgins obviously thinks that you are the right person for the job. Never feel guilty when opportunities come to you."

Amy smiled and finished her orange juice. She stayed another hour before heading home.

"Thank you for a lovely evening everyone. I will see you at work tomorrow."

"Bye Amy."

Amy arrived home to the sound of voices coming from the kitchen. Amy went to see who it was.

"Tara!" Amy shrilled as they rushed to each other. "What are you doing here?"

"That's a charming welcome!" Tara laughed.

"I will leave you girls to catch up. Time for bed," said Amy's foster mother.

"Good night, Mum. Sleep well."

"Good night Mrs R." Tara waved.

Amy's mother left the room and Amy and Tara sat down at the table. "Tea?" said Amy.

"A Brandy would be good." Tara smiled knowing that Amy did not approve of alcohol.

"Is everything okay, Tara, why are you back so soon?"

"Amy, I just wanted to surprise you."

"Tara!?"

"I have left the cruise ship."

"Why?" said Amy. "You love working there."

"I sort of got involved with someone."

"And?" said Amy.

"It was one of the passengers."

"Is there a problem with that?"

"Kind of," Tara replied.

"Tara, what do you mean by kind of?"

"He was there with his wife!"

"Tara!" roared Amy...

"Amy, I could not help myself."

"And what happened?" said Amy.

"Well, his wife found us together."

"What do you mean by 'together'?"

"You know...together!"

"Oh Tara, what is wrong with you?"

"Well, she complained to the captain and, of course, I got the sack... and here I am."

"Tara Smith you are an absolute nightmare," Amy scolded.

"I know, but you love me!" Tara laughed.

"So, what are you going to do now?"

"I will get a singing job in one of the local clubs or pubs for the time being and take it from there."

"What am I going to do with you?" Amy smiled.

"Well, you can let me stay here for a while? Just until I find a place to live?" Tara said in a cheeky way.

"Tara, you are always welcome here."

"You are the best, Amy."

"Of course, I am." They both laughed.

***

The next morning Amy was up bright and early making breakfast.

"Morning," a bleary-eyed Tara said.

"Morning Tara, did you sleep well?"

"I certainly did. Why are you up so early?" Tara asked.

"I have to go to work, and you can start looking for a job!"

"I have only been back one day. At least let me have a few days off!"

"Okay, then you start looking."

"I will. Amy, you are a slave driver!" Tara laughed.

"I will be home at six o clock. And please do not get into any trouble."

"Yes Mum," Tara said sarcastically.

Tara cleared the breakfast things away and went for a soak in the bath.

What should I do now? Tara thought. *I will surprise Amy with a home cooked dinner.*

Not being the best at cooking, Tara never cooked. She looked for a very easy meal. Deciding on Spaghetti Bolognaise, Tara went to buy the ingredients and started her preparation.

Amy was extremely busy at work and was looking forward to getting home to see Tara and hearing all about her adventures. Now Amy had to tell Tara that she was no longer with Luke.

"Hello, anyone home?" Amy called out.

"In the kitchen," Tara hollered.

"Something smells good." Amy walked into the kitchen and stood still in her tracks. The kitchen was in total shambles. Poor Tara looked like she'd had a fight with the Bolognese sauce. Amy put her hand to her mouth so not to laugh.

"Welcome home," Tara smiled. "I cooked for you," she said, feeling proud of herself.

"I can see that. What are we having?" Amy asked.

"Spaghetti Bolognese, but it does not look right?" Tara said confused.

Amy could not hold back any longer and burst into laughter.

"Amy, why are you laughing? It took me all day to cook, and I made the sauce from scratch."

"Tara, it looks fine. Let me taste it." Amy said, as she dipped a spoon into the bolognaise to try it. "Actually, it is quite good. It just needs a bit more seasoning." Amy added a bit more salt and pepper. "It is perfect," she smiled. "And you said you could not cook!"

"This is the first and last time. It is hard work," Tara blurted.

"Thank you, Tara. I do appreciate what you have done, it was a lovely surprise. Tomorrow, it is a Chinese takeaway!"

Tara looked at Amy and burst into laughter.

After dinner, Tara washed the dishes and made Amy a cup of tea.

"I like this. You can come again!" Amy smiled.

"How was your day?" Tara asked.

"It was very busy, but it is always like that. I have never worked so hard since taking on this new role."

"Well, this weekend I am taking you out, and we are going to relax and have a good time," Tara suggested.

"That will be wonderful Tara." Then the question came.

"Is Luke coming over tonight? It would be good to see him."

"Luke and I kind of split up."

"What do you mean split up?" Tara asked.

"Luke ended the relationship. He felt we were drifting apart, and I guess we were."

"But you have been together for so long."

"I know, but to be honest, I am glad that we have."

"Amy. You didn't tell him, did you?"

"No, I did not feel comfortable. Tara, you know I find it difficult to talk about."

"Amy, not all men are like your Dad. Luke would have made you happy."

"I know. But I would not have made him happy."

"Amy, it is time to stop living in the past and move on."

"Move on? I live with this nightmare day in and day out," Amy cried.

"Then get some help. Amy they are dead, but you are still alive. Do not let that man ruin your life too."

Amy became very tearful and broke down crying in Tara's arms. It was easy for Tara to say this, but for Amy, it was the very thing she had tried to hide from for years.

Chapter 5

Amy felt more relaxed now that she had told Tara about her split up with Luke. But still the nightmares continued.

Tara finally found a job, singing in a nearby pub, and eventually a place of her own to live too.

"Amy, what do you have planned on Friday night?" asked Tara as she was brushing her hair.

"Nothing really, why?"

"Come to the pub and watch me sing, invite some of your work friends."

"I am not keen on going to the pub, Tara."

"I know, but you really do need to get out more, and what better time than to come and see me, your best friend, making a fool of herself?" Tara grinned.

"Exactly, I want to keep my friends thank you very much," Amy smirked.

"Amy, that is so rude of you!"

Amy looked at Tara and chuckled. "Of course I will come and watch you sing. What kind of friend would I be if I did not, but, I will not be making a habit of it, so you better sing well."

"You can be so brutal Amy."

"You're welcome." They both roared with laughter.

Amy was a bit nervous asking her work colleagues to go out for the evening. They usually invited Amy.

"We would like that Amy. To be honest, I am a bit surprised you asked, seeing you are not a pub person," Gill said.

"Tara insisted. She suggested that it would be good to ask all of you too," Amy smiled.

"It is going to be a good night; I have not seen a live singer for a while. What kind of songs does Tara sing?" asked Matt, another one of Amy's colleagues.

"I have no idea Matt. This will be the first time I have seen Tara sing professionally."

"Is she hot?" grinned Matt.

"Matt you cannot ask things like that," sighed Gill.

Amy laughed. "You will see for yourself on Friday."

***

Back at home, Amy was getting ready for her night out. "You look gorgeous Amy." Mum started coughing.

"You have had that cough for a while now, maybe you need to see the doctor?"

"I am fine Amy, probably just a virus. I am going to have an early night. You have a good evening; Tara will be wonderful."

Mum took herself off to bed and Amy continued getting ready.

Amy arrived at the pub feeling slightly uncomfortable. She was not used to going to a pub on her own.

"Amy!" Tara shrieked. "You came!"

"Of course I did! I would not miss your big night. You look amazing Tara. How are you feeling?"

"A bit nervous, but nothing a few more brandies won't fix."

"You drink too much Tara."

"Amy, I love you dearly, but I can do without your motherly advice tonight, thank you. Where are your friends? I am looking forward to meeting them."

"They will be here soon."

Just as Amy said that her friends arrived.

"I have to go and prepare my voice. I will see you during the break." Tara ran off backstage.

Amy and her friends were having a really good time singing and clapping their hands. When there was a break, Tara came over as promised. Amy introduced Tara to her friends.

"Are you enjoying the show?" Tara asked.

"Absolutely," said Matt enthusiastically.

"I aim to please everyone," Tara beamed with her flirtatious smile.

Amy playfully shook her head.

"Amy I will be going to a party after the show. Do you want to come?"

"Tara, I think you know my answer to that!"

"Of course I do. I have to get back on stage, I will come and say goodbye when I finish."

Amy and her friends continued enjoying the rest of the show.

"Amy, that was an amazing night; we must do it again soon. Tara is awesome." Matt danced around like an excited child. The rest of the group laughed.

"Someone has a little crush on a certain singer," Amy smiled.

"Come on Casanova, time to go home." Gill held a drunk Matt

by the arm and led him to the door.

"Goodnight everyone, see you on Monday," Amy waved.

Amy found Tara chatting with some fans. "Excuse me Tara." Tara turned around and put her arm around Amy.

"Amy, my best friend in the whole world, did you like my singing?"

"I did, very much Tara. You are good at this," Amy smiled.

"Thank you, I think so too!"

"I am going home now, enjoy the party. I will talk to you tomorrow."

"I adore you Amy."

"I love you too, Tara."

***

Amy woke up the next morning feeling bright and cheerful. She had enjoyed the evening out the night before more than she had expected.

Mum entered the kitchen and was still coughing. "You need to see the doctor about that cough," Amy suggested.

"I am going to make an appointment today," Amy's mum replied. "Amy, I wanted to talk to you. You have been living with me for a long time now, longer than any other foster child I have had. Do you ever think about wanting to move into your own home?"

"No," said Amy, looking puzzled. "Do you not want me here anymore?"

"Yes, of course I do. But when a child reaches adulthood, they are usually ready to move on. That is what being a foster parent is. We only have you live with us until you are either adopted or at the age where you are able to look after yourself."

Amy looked upset. "I like living with you. This is my home. I do not want to live anywhere else."

"You are sweet Amy. I remember that frightened little girl that arrived to us all those years ago. Look at you now, a delightful young woman."

"Then let me stay."

"Amy, I was not saying you had to leave, I just wanted you to know that you are free to go at any time. I will be taking retirement soon and I do not want to be a burden to you."

"I have lived here for half of my life. You have taken care of me. It is my turn to take care of you," Amy whispered.

"Amy, I love you just like all of my other foster children, but you seem to tug at my heart more than anyone else."

"So, can I stay?"

"As long as you wish," she smiled.

Amy threw her arms around her Mum. "I love you."

"I love you too Amy."

Amy was so happy. She had an amazing job, a loving home, and the best friend in the world, but was concerned about the persistent rasping cough her mum had.

After having several appointments and tests, Amy and her mum received some devastating news.

"Mrs Robins, looking at your test results and screenings, we found that you have a tumour on one of your lungs."

"What do you mean a tumour? Mum only has a cough."

"Your mother has a chronic cough, meaning that she has had it for longer than eight weeks, which will also explain the tiredness, dizzy spells, infection and chest pains."

"What are you talking about, Mum never had any of those symptoms, I would have noticed. I know she was feeling tired a lot but that was all."

The consultant looked at Amy's mum.

"Amy I am sorry. I did not want you to worry."

Amy could not believe what she was hearing.

Amy and her mum left the hospital in a state of shock. When they arrived home, Mum went up to her bedroom to rest. Amy sat in the lounge, buried her head in her hands and sobbed.

Tara raced to see Amy. "Amy, I am so sorry." And gave her the biggest hug. "Is there anything I can do, how is Mrs R?"

"There is not anything anyone can do. Mum needs time to process it all. I just have to make sure she is comfortable and be here for her."

"Cancer, I cannot believe it. Mrs R has always been active and healthy."

"Nine months Tara. That is what the consultant said. What am I going to do without her?" Amy broke down in tears. Tara held Amy close in her arms and let her cry.

***

Over the next few months, Mum put all her affairs in place. Amy took an extended leave from work to look after her.

Amy and Mum spent every minute together exploring and having the best adventures.

Amy informed all the children she could find that Mum and Dad had fostered over the years. Many of them came to see Mum, knowing that it would be their last time.

Mum was getting weaker each day. Amy arranged for a special bed to be put in the lounge, so Mum did not have to climb the stairs. Amy would take her for small walks around the garden until she had no strength left. A specialist nurse would come every day to check on Mum.

"Amy," Mum whispered as she lay in Amy's arms. "Promise me there will be no fuss. I want you all to remember the good times and to be happy."

Amy tried so hard to hold back the tears. "How about I read you your favourite book?" Amy had only gotten to the second page when she heard her mum sigh. Amy knew she had passed away. Putting the book down Amy stroked her mum's hair. "Sleep peacefully Mum, I love you."

Amy kissed her Mum gently on the forehead as tears streamed down her face.

Chapter 6

It was the day of the funeral and a gloriously sunny day. Amy looked out of the window reflecting on her time growing up with her foster parents and how happy and grateful she was to them.

"Amy, are you OK?" Tara whispered.

"I have to be Tara. When my real parents and Josh died, my world ended. Living with people I do not know feeling scared and alone. It took me a long time to settle into a new home with foster parents and other children. I hated every minute of it. When my nightmares began, Mum came into my bedroom, held my hand, and stroked my forehead until I fell back to sleep, and she continued to do that even as I grew into an adult. She would always say to me, 'You are never too old to have the touch of a hand and the love of a heart to bring you comfort and reassurance.'"

"That is lovely Amy," Tara wept, wiping a tear from her eye.

"I feel like that little girl again, scared and alone."

Tara held Amy by the hand and gave her a reassuring smile.

***

When Amy and Tara arrived at the cemetery, Amy was pleased that plenty of people came to pay their respects and to see all of those many children that Mum and Dad had fostered over the years. Mum's request was not to have a church service and to have as little fuss as possible.

She would be proud with how it was arranged, Amy thought.

When the service was over, Amy spent a few minutes by herself at the graveside. "Thank you, Mum, for everything you did for me. I will never forget you."

Amy went and placed two roses on the headstone of her birth mother and brother, Josh. "I miss you both so much Mum. But I swear, until the day I die, I will never forgive the man who snatched you both away from me."

Amy walked off, head held high, wiping the tears from her face.

After a few weeks, Amy received a letter from her foster mother's solicitor asking her to come to his office.

"Tara, will you come with me to see Mum's solicitor? I do not want to go by myself."

"Of course, I will; what do you think it is about?"

"I guess we will find out when we get there," Amy muttered.

Amy and Tara arrived at the solicitors. The receptionist asked them to sit down in the waiting area. A tall man with a funny-looking moustache came to meet them.

"Hello, my name is Mr Jenkins. Please, come into my office."

Amy was feeling very nervous and was not sure what to expect.

"Mrs Robins came to see me a few months before she died and instructed me to amend her will. She asked that you be here."

Tara and Amy looked at each other. Mr Jenkins read the will to Amy.

"Mrs Robins asked me to first say that she loved you very much and how proud of you she was."

A tear trickled down Amy's cheek. Amy brushed it away gently and Tara held her by the hand.

"Your foster mother had no children of her own or living family. In her words, she stated: 'Amy was the oldest child that we cared for, and the daughter I always wanted. Many children came to live with us. Amy was the one I wished that I had adopted as my own. Therefore, I leave my estate to her.'"

Amy looked at Tara in shock.

Mr Jenkins continued. "I leave my house and all the contents to Amy, plus my finances."

"How much did she leave?" asked Tara.

Mr Jenkins scrolled through his papers. "Mrs Robins left three hundred and fifty thousand pounds."

"Shut the front door!" squealed Tara putting her hand over her mouth.

Amy sat there in silence.

"I just need you to sign some papers, and everything is yours."

Amy and Tara left the solicitors in a state of shock.

"Time for a drink," Tara remarked.

"Do you know what? I will join you."

"Amy, you do not drink." Tara laughed.

"Well, today, I do. Are you coming?" Amy headed off towards the pub.

This really was out of character for Amy, and Tara was quite concerned.

Tara ordered a brandy for herself and an orange juice for Amy. Tara placed the drinks on the table. Amy picked up the glass of brandy and drank it in one go, nearly bringing it back up. "Oh my God, Amy, what are you doing?"

"Another one," Amy ordered.

"No. I am taking you home."

"Tara, I love you, but please butt out. Where is that brandy?" Amy demanded.

"You are going to regret this in the morning," Amy warned.

***

Amy woke up the next day with the biggest hangover. "Morning," said Tara. "And how are we feeling?"

"I do not feel good at all," Amy moaned.

"Sit down and have a cup of coffee. What on earth came over you, Amy?"

"I really do not understand it myself, Tara. Something just snapped inside me."

"But why drink alcohol? That is the one thing that you are so against."

"Now I know why. Tara, I have to go." Feeling unwell, Amy ran to the bathroom.

Tara checked on Amy and helped her back to bed and left her to sleep.

Later that evening, Amy was starting to feel a bit better. She took a shower and drank lots of water. Tara came and sat beside her.

"Well young lady, what was that all about?"

"I really do not know Tara. I am so disappointed in myself, drinking alcohol. What on earth was I thinking? I cannot bare it with a passion."

"Exactly, that is what I do not understand why you did it?"

"Everything just got to me. Everyone I care about has gone."

"You still have me Amy, and I am not going anywhere."

"Yes, I do have you Tara. The best friend anyone can ever wish for."

"Next time, do not turn to alcohol." Tara laughed.

"Do not worry, there will not be a next time, I can guarantee that!"

***

Amy returned to work after her extended leave. Feeling a little anxious, she took a deep breath before walking into the office.

"Amy, welcome back. How are you?" Gill gave Amy a hug. "We were so sorry to hear about your mum."

"Thank you, Gill. I am OK, better than I was. I just want to get back to work. And I can see there are plenty of things for me to do," said Amy smiling, looking at the piles of files on her desk.

Amy's boss Mr Higgins called her into his office. "It is good to have you back. How are you?"

"I am good. Thank you for sending flowers and for letting me have so much time off of work. I see there is a lot to catch up with."

"Take it one day at a time Amy and work your way through the best that you can."

At the end of the day, Amy felt exhausted. All she wanted to do was go home and sleep, but first she had to speak with Tara.

When Amy arrived home, she called Tara. "Can you come over? I want to talk to you."

"Sure, is everything okay?"

"Yes fine, I just want to ask you something."

"I will be there soon."

Tara left immediately.

"How was your first day back at work?"

"I am exhausted, there is a lot for me to catch up with. Everyone was so welcoming and lovely. It will take a few days to get back into the swing of things."

"So, what do you want to talk to me about?" asked Tara eagerly.

"How would you feel about moving in with me? The house is a bit big for me to live in and I can do with the company."

"Really?" Tara shrieked. "I would love that Amy! I am going to be the best housemate ever. We shall have so much fun."

"I am regretting it already," Amy laughed.

"When can I move in?"

"Whenever you want to Tara." Amy handed her a set of house keys.

"I am going to go and pack. I will be back within an hour."

Tara rushed out of the door then turned back.

Tara kissed Amy and gave her the biggest hug. "Love you. See you soon."

"I love you too..." But Tara was already out the door. Amy smiled and laid her head down on the sofa, drifting off to sleep.

Chapter 7

"It is amazing to live here with you Amy. Can you believe that after all these years I would end up moving in? Imagine what Mrs R would say."

"Mum will be up in heaven saying, 'Tara, you are the untidiest person I know.'"

"Amy, that is so not true." Amy looked at Tara. "OK, I am," Tara admitted. They both were in fits of giggles.

"Amy, have you any thoughts about what you will do with all that money Mrs R left to you?"

"To be honest, no. Maybe I will invest in something. I have never had so much. I am still very shocked that Mum left me everything."

"Mrs R was very generous to you. If you require assistance, I would be happy to help." Tara grinned.

"I bet you are," laughed Amy, throwing a cushion at Tara.

It had been a difficult time for Amy, and she needed a break to rest and relax.

Summer was almost here and Amy decided to take a week's holiday."

So, what are you planning to do on your week off from work?" Tara asked.

"I am going to take each day as it comes. I just want to take things easy and refresh after the past months."

"Amy, I heard you last night crying and shouting, was it a nightmare?"

"Yes. Since my foster mother died, they have gotten worse."

"I am not surprised Amy; it has been a roller coaster of emotions... This holiday will do you good."

***

The first day of Amy's holiday was a delightful sunny day. Perfect to be by the lake and read a book. Amy took a blanket to sit on and a bottle filled with cold coconut water. Finding the ideal spot, Amy placed her blanket on the ground and rubbed suntan lotion onto her skin. Amy got comfortable and started to read the book.

Whilst enjoying soaking up the glorious sunshine and reading her book, an excited dog jumped into the lake, making Amy rather wet.

"Really?" Amy shouted, getting up from the ground.

"Sorry," came a voice from behind her. "Sam come here now." The dog bounded up to its owner shaking the water from his fur, making Amy even more wet. "Sam, No. Please forgive my dog. He gets very excited when he is around the lake."

"Maybe you should consider keeping him on a lead," Amy scoffed as she wiped herself down.

"I can only apologise again. Please, let me buy you a coffee, and I promise to put Sam on his leash."

"There is no need to do that, I will dry off on my way home."

"Please, I would like to."

Amy politely refused and started to walk away.

"The coffee shop is on the way out of the park so you may as well dry off in the sun."

Amy stopped and turned around.

"One coffee and then I am leaving."

Tony smiled and put the leash on Sam and headed to the coffee shop. "Do you come here often?"

Amy looked at him and laughed.

"Sorry, that sounded like a chat up line, it was not meant to be. That was awkward," he said shyly.

Amy smiled. "The answer to your question is no, I have only been here a few times. I have a week's holiday, so I thought I would come and relax in the sunshine."

"And then we came along and ruined your time. I am really sorry Sam soaked you."

"It is only water, and I am almost dry. So, besides buying strange ladies' coffee, what is your line of work?"

"I have my own marketing company. I design marketing materials for websites and presentations, email campaigns and social media."

"That sound's busy," Amy remarked.

"It is. What is your job?"

"I am a legal personal assistant for a corporate law solicitor."

"That is very impressive."

"It is a lot of paperwork." Amy smiled. "Is that the time?" Amy glanced at her watch. "Thank you for the coffee. It has been an eventful morning!"

"Thank you for allowing me to buy you coffee as my way of an apology."

"Goodbye, and keep Sam on the lead in the park, otherwise you will be buying a lot of people coffee." Amy turned away and grinned.

***

"Hey, how was your trip to the park?" asked Tara.

"It was lovely until a dog jumped into the lake and soaked me. And his owner bought me a coffee to apologise."

Tara laughed. "You do look a bit bedraggled. Hang on, owner, coffee?" Tara's face lit up.

"It was just a coffee Tara, nothing more than that."

"And does the owner have a name?"

"His name is Tony, and he owns a marketing company. The dog is Sam. And before you ask, no, I am not seeing him again!"

"That is a shame. You could do with a man in your life."

"Tara, the last thing that I want, or need, is a man in my life. You should know this by now." Amy looked at Tara in a stern way.

"I am going to have a shower and get into some comfortable clothes."

"I am going to wash that man right out of my hair," Tara sang teasing Amy.

***

Refreshed after having her shower, Amy made herself a sandwich and coffee and sat at the kitchen table with an art magazine.

"Art? Since when have you been interested in paintings?" Tara remarked, looking over Amy's shoulder.

"I am going to the art gallery tomorrow. It will be good to get myself familiar with different types of painting techniques and portraits."

"Amy, you do not have a clue about art," Tara mocked.

"That is why I am reading this magazine, so I have some knowledge before I go. It would not do you any harm to come and educate yourself."

"I get all the education I need when I look at the people that come into the pub," Tara giggled.

Amy could not help but smile.

"Amy, how about we get a takeaway, a bottle of wine and watch a chick flick tonight?"

Amy glared at Tara.

"What? OK, not the wine."

"That would be lovely. But I am choosing the film," Amy insisted.

"Fine," Tara sulked.

***

After breakfast the following morning, Amy made her way to the art gallery.

The gallery was quite busy, with a lot of tourists being escorted around by a guide. Amy was a bit cheeky and tagged onto the end of the group. At least that way she would understand a bit more about art. Amy found this new experience fascinating.

Walking around the gallery, a painting caught Amy's eye. She quietly slipped away from the group to check it out. The colours were vibrant and bright. Amy slowly stepped back to get a better view of it and bumped into someone.

"I am so sorry," said Amy apologetically. They both turned around at the same time.

"Amy, what a surprise. How are you?"

"Tony, you are the last person I expected to see."

"I could say the same thing. Do you come here often?"

Amy laughed. Tony looked puzzled. "Have I said something amusing?"

"You asked me that at the park."

"So, I did." Tony felt embarrassed. "There is a very good restaurant just around the corner. Would you like to have lunch with me? That is if you have finished here."

"I was just going to grab a sandwich."

"I understand, maybe another time. It was good to see you again Amy," Tony said as he started to turn away.

"Actually–" Amy paused for a second. "I would like that."

They went to a little Italian restaurant called Carlos. Amy admired the decor. "It looks very elegant," she said.

"Yes, it is a lovely place. I come here to escape when I want peace and quiet. And when I am hungry, of course." Tony smiled.

The waitress brought over the menu. "Amy would you like wine with your meal?"

"No, thank you, I do not drink. A sparkling water would be good."

"Make that two sparkling waters please. I avoid alcohol as well. I have never found it necessary to be honest." This made Amy smile inside.

"What do you like to do for entertainment? Besides going to parks, getting soaked by crazy dogs and art galleries?" Tony inquired, in an attempt to get to know her better.

"I really enjoy simple things; walking in nature, watching films, reading. To be honest, this is the first time I have been to an art gallery and I found it rather enlightening. Maybe this will be a new activity. What do you like doing?"

"Much of the same thing. I work long hours, so that keeps me busy."

"What would you like to order?" asked the waitress.

"Amy?"

"I will have the Pasta Puttanesca please."

"And I would like the Pepperoni Fettuccine." Tony turned his attention back to Amy. "I remember you saying that you are on holiday now. What else do you have planned?"

"I have not really thought about it to be honest."

"The zoo is a cool place to visit," Tony mentioned.

Amy laughed. "I guess it is. I have not been to one since I was a child."

"You should go. I can always accompany you. It will be fun," Tony suggested.

Amy found herself staring into Tony's eyes. *What was it about him that made her feel safe?*

"Amy, are you OK?" Tony asked concerned.

"Yes, sorry. The zoo sounds like a good idea."

"How about tomorrow? I just happen to have the day off."

Amy smiled. "I would like that."

Amy and Tony finished their meal and left the restaurant. "I will pick you up at ten thirty in the morning," said Tony, with a smile on his face.

"I look forward to it! Bye." Amy started walking away, feeling giddy like a schoolgirl.

"Amy?" Tony called. "You haven't told me where you live?"

Amy stopped and turned back around, blushing as she did so. Tony offered her his phone and she wrote down her address on a memo before passing it back. "See you tomorrow," Tony smiled. Amy waved awkwardly and hurried off.

***

Amy returned home with a smile on her face.

"Someone looks happy," Tara remarked as Amy came into the house.

"Do I?" Amy smiled again.

"Yes, you have a rosy glow on your cheeks... Are you sure you went to the art gallery?" Tara teased accusatorily.

"I certainly did. It was very entertaining."

"Art gallery, entertaining?" Tara mocked. "Amy, you are not telling me something."

"What do you mean!"

"Amy, tell me." Tara insisted.

Amy sighed as she decided to give in. "Well, do you remember when I went to the park yesterday and the dog got me wet? Tony, the dog owner, bought me coffee."

"Yes, I remember."

"Well, I bumped into him, literally, at the gallery. He invited me to lunch. We had a pleasant time and Tony suggested taking me to the zoo tomorrow."

"Slow down. That was one heck of a trip to the art gallery. Amy, you seem a bit smitten?"

"Tara, that is just ridiculous. I enjoy his company. I do not want, or need, a man in my life."

"Who are you kidding? Amy, it is OK to have fun and be happy you know?" Tara wished Amy wasn't so scared to enjoy herself once in a while.

"It is just the zoo, no need to make a big fuss about it," Amy responded sharply.

"Why are you getting agitated and red faced if it is not a big deal?" said Tara exasperated.

"Leave it Tara. I am going to my room."

"Amy, this is silly."

Amy stormed off to her room and did not talk to Tara again that evening.

***

Amy woke up at the crack of dawn. She was so excited about seeing Tony, but after her disagreement with Tara, Amy was not sure that she wanted to go with him to the zoo. Amy got out of bed and went into the kitchen to make coffee.

"What time is it?" yawned Tara, scratching her head.

"Six thirty. Would you like a coffee?"

"Yes please. Amy, are you still mad at me? I did not mean to upset you."

"I apologise Tara, I should not have reacted the way I did. I was embarrassed. Since my relationship ended with Luke, I feel if I'm to let another man into my life, it would end just the same way."

"Amy, you have just met Tony. It is a date to the zoo; you are not getting married. Just take it one day at a time. You were so happy yesterday I have not seen you like that in a very long time."

"Yes, I was happy. Then the realisation of dating and having to explain about my family makes me feel physically sick."

Tara took Amy by the hand. "Someday you are going to have to trust someone and begin trusting yourself. You must think about seeing a councillor, Amy. To hear you at night crying and screaming is heart-breaking. But you have to seek help and start moving forward."

"Yes, I do. But it is so difficult Tara. I tell myself the same thing, but something always stops me."

Tara held Amy in her arms. "You will get there Amy. So, start by getting ready and enjoying a friendly day out at the zoo with Tony and not thinking about the questions he may ask."

Amy looked at Tara and nodded her head in agreement.

Amy had a picnic ready to take to the zoo. It was ten thirty when the doorbell rang.

"I will get it." Tara ran to the door.

"Tara, no." But it was too late.

Tara opened the door and standing there was a very handsome man.

"Hello, you must be Tony. Come in."

"Tony, this is Tara, my housemate."

"Good to meet you Tara." Tony shook her hand. "Amy, you look lovely."

Amy could feel her cheeks blushing.

"Thank you." There was an awkward silence as they gazed at each other.

Tara smiled and slightly chuckled under her breath.

"Have fun!" Tara bellowed ushering Amy and Tony out of the door. She felt like a proud Mum seeing her child off on her first date.

The zoo was very busy with lots of school children there on a day trip. Tony parked the car and walked with Amy to the entrance. He paid at the ticket box and picked up a map of the zoo.

They slowly took their time going from one animal enclosure to the next, laughing and joking.

"Those naughty monkeys, blowing raspberries at you, and the elephant spraying water making you all wet." Amy was crying with laughter. "Karma comes to mind!"

"Point taken." Tony was in stitches, giggling so hard. "I have a towel in the car, I need to dry off. We can get the food at the same time and have lunch."

"That's a good idea." Amy could not stop herself from laughing.

Amy and Tony found a place on the grass to lay their blanket and set out the food. "Between the two of us we can feed an army." Tony smiled. "The sun is glorious." Amy closed her eyes and breathed in deeply. "Lucky I brought the sun cream; your shoulders are getting very red. May I?" Tony started rubbed the cool lotion into Amy's skin, but Amy was feeling uncomfortable and moved away. Tony stopped and put the bottle back in the bag.

Feeling brave, Amy said, "Do you have family Tony?"

"Yes, there is Sam, you have already met him," Tony grinned. "I have an older sister, Gina. She is a dentist. My younger twin brothers Ryan and Ben are at university studying business and accountancy. My mum is a primary school teacher. Dad is in computer programming. We are a mixed bunch really."

"One big happy family," Amy uttered sarcastically, immediately regretting her decision to start a conversation about family.

"Yes, we are." Tony felt that something was not quite right. "Tell me about your family?"

Here we go Amy thought. She could feel the knots in her stomach already. "My Mum and Dad and brother Josh all died. I grew up in a care home from the age of thirteen and then my foster parents died. The only family member that I have now is my best friend Tara, who you met this morning."

Tony did not know what to say. Amy could feel the tears in her eyes. "I am not feeling good. Do you mind if we leave?"

"Of course." Tony packed away the food and blanket and drove Amy home.

"Thank you for a lovely day. I am sorry to leave early. I must have sunstroke."

"There is no need to apologise. The sun was very hot today. Can I see you again?"

"There are things I need to sort out before I go back to work and a lot of paperwork to catch up on. I will call you when things are not so hectic."

"Sure, here is my number. I look forward to hearing from you." Tony bent over to kiss Amy goodbye on the cheek. Amy moved away and got out of the car. She waved and went into the house.

Tony was confused. They were having such a good day until the family conversation. Did he say something wrong? He took one last look at the house and drove away.

Amy entered the house and threw her bags onto the sofa.

"How was your day?" Tara asked enthusiastically.

"It was awful."

"What happened?"

"It was going so well, we were laughing and joking around, sat and had a lovely picnic. My shoulders were quite red from the sun and then Tony rubbed sun cream on them."

"Sounds romantic?" Tara was getting excited.

"I started to feel uncomfortable with Tony doing that. I moved away so he would stop."

"Amy, that was a considerate thing for Tony to do. What was the problem?"

"I got a mental picture of my father laying his hands on Mum. I panicked. But the crazy thing was, I then went and asked about his family."

"What was crazy about that?"

"I knew that the question was going to come about my family."

"Would that have been so wrong?"

"Yes. You know I do not like talking about it."

"So, what did you say?"

"I told him they all died, and you were the only family member I have left. I pretended to feel unwell and wanted to go home. To make matters worse, he went to kiss my cheek when he dropped me off and again, I moved away."

"Amy, you are going to have to talk about this to someone at some point."

"I will. When I am ready."

"Are you going to see Tony again?"

"I'm not sure. I doubt he will be interested in a mad woman."

"You are not mad Amy. Well, maybe a little." Tara laughed attempting to lighten the mood.

"Tara, what am I going to do?"

"I suggest you have a lay down and rest. We can talk later when you are feeling a little less anxious."

"You are right. I am tired."

Amy laid on her bed, but all she could think about was that dreadful night. Eventually she fell asleep.

Amy slept for a few hours. Her shoulders were feeling sore from the sun. She got out of bed and headed to the bathroom to get some cream. On the way, Amy could hear Tara on the phone and then heard the screams. Amy rushed down the stairs.

"Tara, are you OK?"

"Amy, you will never believe it, I have a job!"

"Tara, I know. Singing at the pub."

"No, not that job. A place on a cruise ship."

"Really? I am surprised they invited you back after what happened."

"I know. They just cannot resist me," said Tara excitedly.

"Tara, honestly. When do you leave?"

"The ship sails in two days."

Amy felt her heart drop. "That soon? I am really happy for you Tara, but I will miss you."

Tara suddenly felt a pang of guilt. "I will miss you too Amy, but it will go quickly, and I will be back for Christmas in no time." Tara paused. "Are you feeling better after your sleep?"

"Yes. I am still unsure whether or not to see Tony again though."

"Amy, do you like him?"

"I think so."

"Then see him! Why make yourself miserable? Your Mum and Josh would be disappointed knowing you were putting your life on hold because of what happened."

"It is not that easy Tara."

"Amy, at least try," Tara sighed. "I am going to start packing. Think about it."

Amy knew Tara was right, but could she go through with it?

Chapter 8

"Tara, get a move on, your taxi is here!"

"OK, I am coming."

"Do you have everything?"

"Amy, stop fussing."

"Someone needs to. You are late for everything and you do not want to mess this up again!"

"I am ready. Amy, you had another nightmare last night. Will you please get some help? And free yourself from that prison. Promise me?"

Amy looked at Tara. "I am going to miss you."

"Me too. And stop avoiding the question," Tara scolded.

"Yes, I promise!" Amy gave in.

Tara gave Amy the biggest hug.

"I will see you at Christmas. Love you," she said, as she rushed out the door.

"Love you too."

Amy closed the door and looked around the messy room that Tara had left behind. Amy smiled and got ready for work.

***

"How was your holiday Amy?"

"It was good," Amy replied, looking at the mountain of work on her desk.

"Mr Higgins had an urgent meeting to go to. He asked me to tell you that there are some priority phone calls that need doing before you do anything else." Amy raised her eyebrows. "I am just passing on the message," Gill laughed.

Amy made phone calls and ploughed through work, leaving the office late that evening. All she wanted to do was have a relaxing bath and watch a film with some delicious hot chocolate. Amy was about to get into the bath when there was a knock at the door. Putting on her robe, Amy went and answered it.

"Tony," Amy blushed pulling her robe closer together. "What are you doing here?"

"I was on my way home and wanted to come and say hello."

"Tony, you live in the opposite direction." Tony looked at Amy and smiled awkwardly. "I was about to get into the bath."

"Sorry to turn up unannounced, I will come back another time." Tony started to walk away.

"Tony," Amy called. "You can make us a drink while I get dressed."

Amy got into some comfortable clothes and joined Tony sitting in the lounge.

"How are you?" asked Tony.

"Tired. It has been hectic at work. A lot to catch up with after being away for the week."

"Have you been busy?"

Amy yawned putting her hand over her mouth. "Sorry, it has been a long day."

"Maybe I should go, I can see you are tired. I just wanted to check that things were OK. I have not heard from you?"

"Tony, it has only been a few days, and I am fine."

"I know. I just feel that I have upset you in some way after our trip to the zoo."

Amy was the one now feeling awkward.

"You have not done anything wrong. I had too much sun and it made me feel unwell."

"If you are sure?"

"I am sure," Amy grinned.

"Would you like to go and have dinner?"

"Can we do it another time? I really need to have an early night."

"How about Friday night?" Tony suggested.

Amy hesitated for a minute and remembered what Tara had said to her.

"That will be good."

"I will pick you up seven thirty. Is that OK with you?"

"Yes, I look forward to it."

Amy showed Tony to the door.

"See you on Friday," Tony said, as he left the house.

Amy was exhausted, too tired to even get into her pyjamas. She went upstairs, got into bed and fell straight asleep.

***

Amy woke up early the next morning feeling refreshed after a good sleep. She got up and had a shower, then made coffee and toast before starting her day. The house felt quiet without Tara. Amy was about to get dressed to leave for work when the phone rang.

"Amy, it is me."

"Tara, is everything ok? You only left yesterday."

"Everything is fine, I just wanted to say hello."

"Where are you?"

"Sailing around the island of San Juan, Puerto Rico."

"And you call that work?" mocked Amy.

"I will be singing my heart out later thank you very much. What have you been doing?"

"I went to work after you left, it was extremely busy. Tony came by in the evening."

"Stop there. Tony come over?"

"Yes. He wanted to check that I was OK after my sudden departure from the zoo."

"So, what happened?"

"He asked me out for dinner. I was too tired and declined. And, before you say anything, I am seeing him on Friday."

"I am delighted to hear it. Give yourself a chance and be happy."

"I am happy."

"Amy. You know what I mean."

"Tara, dare I ask, are you behaving yourself?"

"Give me a chance, I have only been here one day. I am just warming up."

"Tara, you are joking?"

Tara laughed so loud.

"Amy, of course I am. I have learned since last time. I just have to make sure I do not get caught next time!"

"Tara, that is not amusing."

"Amy it is so easy to tease you. I must go now. The production manager is calling me for a rehearsal. I will phone you again soon. Love you."

"Love you too."

Amy put the phone down and looked at the clock. *I am going to be late* thought Amy. Amy quickly got dressed, picked up her bag and left for work.

Chapter 9

Friday was finally here, and Amy was looking forward to the weekend after a long and tiring week.

"Amy we are going to the pub. Are you coming?" one of her colleagues asked.

"Not tonight thanks. I am having a relaxing night in. Have a good weekend. See you on Monday."

Amy had forgotten about her date with Tony. She was already settled in watching a film when there was a knock at the door.

Tony was standing there with a bunch of flowers and looking dashing. Then Amy remembered.

"Tony come in. The flowers are lovely! Thank you. Please, sit down, I am nearly ready."

Thankfully Amy was still in her work clothes and looked smartly dressed. She went into the bathroom, brushed her teeth, sprayed a little perfume, and tidied her hair.

"Sorry to keep you waiting," Amy said apologetically putting her coat on.

"You are looking radiant," Tony gushed.

"Thank you." If only he knew that she had forgotten.

"Do you like fish?" Tony asked.

"Yes, I love fish."

"I know a quaint restaurant that serve the best lobster in town and it is within walking distance from here."

Amy nodded in agreement, and they made their way to the

restaurant.

When they arrived at the restaurant they were shown to their table.

"What would you like to drink Amy?"

"The sparkling water will be fine, thank you."

"Shall we have the lobster special?" Tony suggested.

"That will be good."

Tony gave the order to the serving waitress; "Two sparkling waters and the lobster special please."

"How has your week been Amy?"

"There was a lot for me to catch up with after my holiday, so a lot of late nights at the office. I managed to get it all finished thankfully." Amy paused. "How about you? Tell me more about the marketing you do."

"I provide a service to help companies market their business in a more beneficial way to grow and give their clients and customers better value whether that be through social media, email, or presentations. I have been building my company for the last five years and after many a sleepless night I am finally where I want to be."

"And where is that exactly?"

"To be at the top of my profession and gaining credibility. I believe I have now achieved that."

"Hard work pays off. Well done." Amy was impressed.

Amy and Tony were having a pleasant evening enjoying each other's company and getting to know one another better. Eventually, it was time to leave the restaurant. Tony walked Amy back to her house and they chatted more along the way.

"What are your plans for the weekend?" inquired Tony.

"Tomorrow I am going to the museum and on Sunday I am having a day at home doing my washing and housework. Nothing exhilarating," Amy replied. "Do you have plans?"

"I am going to take Sam and visit my parents. Otherwise, not very much."

"Would you like to come by for a coffee Sunday on the way back from your parents?"

"I would like that," Tony replied, finally feeling like he was getting somewhere with Amy.

"Thank you, Tony, for a lovely evening." Amy smiled, feeling warm inside.

"Thank you, Amy, for being a delightful companion. See you on Sunday."

Tony went to kiss Amy on the cheek but pulled back remembering what happened the last time.

Amy went into the house with a big grin on her face. But Amy was still holding her feelings back.

***

Amy was enjoying her visit to the Environmental Museum and was fascinated with the amount of information provided. She learnt about how to help keep the planet safe and protected, and there were lots of fun activities for children to explore.

Amy was getting hungry. She found a cafe not far from the museum. The waitress came to take Amy's order.

"I will have a latte and a ham salad roll please."

While waiting for her food and drink to arrive, Amy's phone rang.

"Amy, how are you?"

"Who is this?"

"Amy, it is Luke."

"Luke. You are the last person I expected to call me," Amy said surprised.

"It is lovely to speak with you too Amy," Luke responded sarcastically.

"I am sorry Luke; it has taken me by surprise. How are you?"

"I am really well. I found your number on my phone and wanted to say hello."

"It has been years Luke. Are you still a carpenter?"

"No, I gave up and found something more inspiring."

The waitresses came over with Amy's order.

"Thank you."

"Amy, where are you?"

"I am in a cafe called Sally's around the corner of the Hampton Museum."

"Wait there, I am not far away. It will be good to see you."

"Luke—" He had already hung up.

Amy was feeling nervous. It has been a very long time since she saw Luke. Ten minutes later Luke arrived. Amy forgot how handsome he was.

"Amy, it is good to see you." Luke lent over and kissed Amy on the cheek. "It has been a long time. You are looking as stunning as ever."

"Luke, you have not changed one bit."

"Just as handsome you mean?" Amy smiled.

"What are you doing. Are you still working at the solicitors?"

"Yes, I am still there," Amy replied. "What is this new inspiring job that you have now?"

"I work for an advertising company."

"What does that involve?"

"I encourage businesses to advertise with us. I love it. I get to meet lots of fascinating people and get loads of free designer clothes and shoes. I have my own flat, a good car, and lots of money in the bank. What more can I ask for?" Luke grinned in a smug way.

"No wonder you love it. And are you in a relationship?"

"No, but I do have a lot of lady friends. You know what I mean." Luke winked at Amy.

What an arrogant pig, Amy thought.

"Is there someone special in your life beside Tara?" Luke uttered. "How is she?"

"Tara is really good, still singing on the cruise ships, travelling all around the world. And no, there is nobody special in my life," Amy said, deciding she wouldn't mention Tony. *They hadn't even kissed, after all.*

"You are still waiting for Mr Right to come along then?" Luke grinned.

Amy ignored Luke's comment, she was starting to get agitated and didn't understand why Luke was bothering her anyway.

"Luke it has been lovely to see you, but I really must be going now."

Luke got out of his chair.

"It was good catching up Amy. We must do it again sometime." Luke kissed Amy on the cheek.

Amy smiled and could not wait for Luke to leave. Once he had gone she finished her drink and left too.

Amy took a slow walk home. Seeing Luke had made her think about Tony and how much she really did like him. Was he her Mr Right?

***

It was Sunday morning and Amy had finished her washing and housework; she was getting butterflies about seeing Tony. *Pull yourself together Amy, it is only coffee.* The phone rang and it was Tony.

"Amy I am not sure what time I will get there. My Father has fallen and needs to go to the hospital. I will be a bit later coming to see you," Tony explained.

"Tony I am sorry to hear that. How is he?"

"In a lot of pain. He fell from a ladder while putting something away in the cupboard. He is just badly bruised, but I would like the doctor to see him."

"Of course, I understand. What if I cook dinner?"

"I would like that. I must go now, see you later," Tony said as he hung up.

Amy knew exactly what she was going to cook and went to buy some ingredients. When she arrived back from the shops she prepared the casserole and cooked it in the slow cooker, then settled down and watched a film. By this time, it was late in the afternoon.

Amy had nodded off whilst watching the film and was woken by a knock on the door. Rubbing her eyes and making herself look presentable, Amy opened the door.

"Tony, you came early."

"We were surprisingly very quick at the hospital."

"How is your Dad?"

"Just bruised, nothing is broken thankfully. He lost his balance and fell from the ladder. It could have been worse," Tony explained, "I hope it is OK for me to come a bit earlier than expected?"

"Of course, I was just watching a film. Actually, I fell asleep."

"It must have been a good film!" smiled Tony. "Something smells lovely."

"I hope you like casserole. It has been in the slow cooker for hours. We can have it now if you are hungry?"

"That sounds perfect. I did not get much time to eat with everything going on with Dad." Tony looked at the food eagerly. "Let me help with something."

"The cutlery is in that drawer. If you can lay the table that will be helpful and there are some elder flower drinks in the fridge and the glasses in the top cupboard."

Amy was feeling relaxed and peaceful as they were chatting over dinner.

"Amy that was delicious. The best casserole I have had in a very long time."

"Thank you. My mum used to make it when I was a child." Amy thought back to her mum and instantly felt a slight sadness creep in.

"What was your mum like?" Tony pressed, but Amy started to

feel an uneasiness wash over her at his questioning.

"You know, just like any mum really," she said, ending the subject.

Amy started to clear the plates from the table. Tony could see Amy was not comfortable talking about her mum so he decided not to push any further.

"I will wash up," Tony offered.

"You do not have to do that, you are my guest."

"And you cooked," Tony said smiling, as he got up to do the dishes.

The night continued and they talked for hours.

"I think it is time that I left, we both have to be up early tomorrow for work. I had a lovely time Amy. Maybe next time I can cook for you?"

"I would like that," Amy said with a warm glow.

Tony lent forward and kissed Amy on the cheek. This time Amy did not pull away.

"I will call you in the week."

Amy waved goodbye to Tony and closed the door. She stood there touching her cheek where Tony had kissed her, sending butterflies through her stomach.

On his drive home Tony thought more about Amy and her guarded behaviour whenever he asked about her family. *Why did she feel uncomfortable talking about her family? What was she hiding?*

Chapter 10

Over the next few weeks Amy and Tony's relationship got stronger every day. They had gone from the friend zone to romance and were enjoying every moment together.

It was getting closer to Christmas. Amy was so looking forward to Tara coming home. And then she got the phone call. Tara was going to be delayed and would be back for New Year instead.

Tony knew Amy would be disappointed that Tara would not be home for Christmas and he wanted to do something to cheer her up.

"Amy, how would you like to go away for a few days over Christmas, just you and me, well, and Sam of course? There is a lovely log cabin in the mountains that sounds so peaceful."

"Tony I would love to, but what about your family? They will expect you to see them at Christmas."

"I will see them at New Year. Tara will be back by then and you will have lots to catch up on."

Amy was so excited but also nervous. She needed to speak with Tara. Amy picked up the phone and dialled her number.

"Amy, are you OK?"

"I need your advice."

"I am always ready to give advice. You know me!" Tara laughed.

"Seriously Tara. Tony has booked us a mini break over Christmas!" Amy panicked.

"What is the problem?"

"I have never stayed alone with a man at night before. Not even all the time I was with Luke."

"Amy. Tony is a lovely man, and he would never take advantage of you."

"I know he is Tara and I trust him more than anyone, besides you, of course. I am just worried about my nightmares," Amy threated.

"Amy it is about time you told Tony. You will not get any help so talk to him. He will understand. Stop thinking about it and just tell him."

"I do not know if I am ready."

"Amy when will you ever be ready? Tony may be the key to unlock you from that prison within. He adores you. You must let a man into your life at some point. Tony is perfect for you. So go and have a wonderful time," Tara scolded.

"You're right Tara, it's time."

"I am always right," Tara stated matter-of-factly.

"Tara. You make me laugh." Amy smiled.

"I know."

Amy and Tara were both laughing by this point.

"Amy, I am going now. Love you."

"I love you too," Amy said as she hung up.

It was two days before Christmas. Tony came bright and early to pick Amy up for their trip.

"Morning gorgeous, are you ready?" Tony asked.

"I sure am." Amy paused. "Hello Sam," she said as she tickled him under his neck. "I know we are going to the mountains. Tell me more."

"All you need to know is that you are going to have a peaceful, relaxing time," Tony grinned, not giving anything away.

"Just what the doctor prescribed," Amy smiled.

Sam barked his agreement.

"See, Sam agrees too."

Amy and Tony laughed with such joy before finally setting off.

The journey took several hours. They finally arrived tired and hungry, but with a beautiful view of the mountainside, its twists and turns, green trees and snowy white tips.

Amy stood there taking in the view.

"Tony this is breath-taking," Amy enthused.

Tony put his arm around Amy in an attempt to get closer, planting a kiss on her cheek. Amy smiled as she felt goosebumps arise at the romance of it all.

"Let us take the suitcases in and have a cup of tea and something to eat," Tony suggested.

The cabin was big and spacious. Plenty of room for an excited Sam to run around.

"This is your room Amy and mine is just next door. Let us unpack and get that fire burning."

Amy made some tea and sandwiches with the provisions they brought with them whilst Tony lit the fire. Amy was already feeling relaxed, and they had only just arrived. She was looking forward to spending time alone with Tony despite her fears. They sat on the floor by the fire to eat their food, whilst Sam circled a spot next to them, plumped himself down and fell asleep.

"This is so peaceful," yawned a tired Amy.

"It is even more picturesque than I imagined when I booked it. The perfect place to unwind." Tony felt pleased at his decision.

"I agree." Amy yawned again, causing Tony to laugh.

"Someone is ready for bed," he said.

"Sorry, the mountain air has already got to me. So, what is the plan for our next few days here?"

"No plan. Take each day as it comes. The idea is to switch off and enjoy our first Christmas together."

"That sounds ideal." Amy was looking forward to it.

After a while the night air became cold, so Tony got Amy a jumper to wear.

"Amy I am taking Sam out for walk before bed. Do you want to come or stay here in the warm?"

"I'll come with you."

Tony let Sam off of his lead to roam around for a bit. Amy and Tony stood under the shining moonlight together.

"Tony, this is wonderful, so quiet. It is as if we are the only ones here." Amy gazed up at the stars.

Tony looked at Amy and pulled her into his arms, making Amy turn her attention to him.

"In this present moment Amy, we *are* the only ones here."

Tony drew Amy in closer and they shared their first proper passionate kiss. Amy felt a rush of emotion as her senses heightened, but her shyness caused her to gently pull away.

"I am feeling quite tired," Amy said awkwardly. "Do you mind if

I go to bed?"

"Not at all, you go on in. I will get Sam," Tony replied, ecstatic he was finally getting somewhere, but slightly disappointed it hadn't gone further.

"See you in the morning."

"Goodnight Amy. Sleep well," Tony said, as Amy went off into the cabin.

Amy got into her pyjamas and snuggled under the duvet. Feeling peaceful, Amy drifted off to sleep.

***

The next morning was Christmas Eve. Amy woke up feeling refreshed after a restful night.

"Good morning sleepyhead." Tony beamed as Amy walked into the kitchen.

"What time is it?"

"It is ten thirty."

"Why did you not wake me up?" Amy asked shocked that she had slept in so late.

"Because you obviously needed to sleep. It was a long day yesterday. Take a seat; I have made breakfast. Pancakes, scrambled eggs, bacon and freshly-made coffee," Tony stated eagerly.

"It all looks delicious. Thank you," Amy said, as she sniffed at the air, taking in the smells.

"How do you feel if we drive to the shops and buy a few Christmas decorations and a small tree?"

"Tony that would be wonderful." Amy was overjoyed. She couldn't wait to make it feel more like Christmas.

"I am going to take Sam for a walk. We can go whenever you are ready."

Amy had never felt so happy as she did right at that moment.

Tony arrived back from his walk with Sam. Amy was ready and excited for their shopping trip, and they set off straight away.

The shops were about a half hour drive from the cabin. The village was not very big but catered for most things.

Tony parked the car. The village was looking very festive with decorations and lights. It had a happy joyful feeling to it.

Amy and Tony had so much fun laughing and joking as they tried on silly masks and hats. They bought lots of food, colourful decorations and lights but had yet to find the perfect tree.

"All this shopping is making me hungry. Let us go to this coffee shop for a drink and a bite to eat," Amy suggested as she led the way. "This has been so much fun. Thank you Tony for this break, it was very much needed."

"You have no need to thank me Amy. Seeing you smile is enough." And he meant it.

After lunch, they searched for the Christmas tree.

"There it is, that is the one!" Amy pointed. Hidden behind the bigger trees stood the perfect one. They bought the tree and loaded the car with their shopping. Just as they were about to leave Amy noticed a group of people sitting in a quiet corner under a big oak tree looking very peaceful and chanting. The smell of roses was coming from that direction. Amy was fascinated and was drawn to go over to them.

"Tony, can we go over to that group of people?" Amy asked.

"Sure. Any particular reason why?"

"I just want to see what they are doing. The aroma of the roses smells glorious."

Amy and Tony made their way over to the group sitting under the tree. An elderly man invited them to sit down. In a quiet voice he explained that they were meditating.

"My name is Spencer. Welcome to our space of tranquillity. Are you familiar with meditation?"

Amy and Tony shook their heads in response to Spencer's question.

"It is a practice aiding the mind, body and soul," Spencer explained. "Focus on mindful breathing; inhaling deeply and exhaling slowly, releasing the things that do not serve us. It has many benefits for our mental health and wellbeing. Reducing stress and helping with emotional balance. The mantra that we are chanting is Om. It connects all living beings to nature and to the universe. Chanting this sound can help to bring peace and calm to the mind, body, and soul. It provides a direct link to the divine and divine knowledge. We may see visions, hear words from the divine spirit, bringing much healing."

Tony and Amy looked at each other fascinated by Spencer's words.

"Feel free to join in. Just close your eyes and take a deep breath in and slowly release whilst listening to the relaxing sound of nature. You can chant the mantra Om out loud or quietly to yourself, or just sit in the silence of peace."

Amy and Tony closed their eyes. Amy began saying the mantra Om quietly to herself, drifting into a calm and peaceful place. After a while Amy opened her eyes and became tearful. Everyone was still in meditation, even Tony. Amy took herself off to one side not wanting to disturb anyone.

Tony opened his eyes to see Amy sitting by herself.

"Are you OK?"

"Yes, I became overwhelmed, and the tears just started flowing. It was very powerful."

"I must say Amy, I have never experienced anything like that before. It was very peaceful. Shall we head back to the cabin now?"

Amy and Tony left quietly and made their way back to the car.

Arriving back to the cabin Amy and Tony were greeted by an excited Sam who jumped up and gave Amy lots of licks making her laugh.

"How about we put the tree and decorations up," Tony suggested, giving Amy a big hug.

Amy smiled lovingly at Tony.

"You know what we need? A good old Christmas song to get us in the spirit." Amy turned on a Christmas song playlist on her phone and they started dancing around. Even Sam joined in barking happily. When the tree and decorations were up Amy stood back and beamed with delight.

"Tony it all looks wonderful. Now it really does feel like Christmas. I think we should cook the turkey this evening then we only have the vegetables to prepare in the morning."

"That sounds like a good plan. Now, you put your feet up whilst I make you a cup of tea and take Sam for a walk and when I get back, we can snuggle up in front of the fire and listen to some more Christmas music."

"That sounds just perfect."

Amy never imagined she could feel so happy. Tony was definitely the right man for her.

The evening was peaceful. The turkey was in the oven. Amy and Tony were snuggled up by the crackling sound of the fire, just enjoying the calmness of the night.

"This has been the best Christmas. Thank you, Tony." Amy smiled warmly.

"Thank you, Amy. For being the most amazing, adorable person that you are. I would not want to be anywhere else but right here with you."

Amy felt like the luckiest lady on the planet, snuggling even closer to Tony, both pf them drifting off to sleep.

Tony woke up suddenly remembering the turkey was still cooking in the oven. He jumped up quickly and removed it. Thankfully it had not burned. Amy stirred from her sleep.

"Is everything OK?"

"Yes, I just rescued the turkey from burning. So we still have dinner for tomorrow," he joked.

Amy got up from the floor and stretched.

"I am going to go to bed now. I will miss it here," she said longingly, knowing their time here would soon come to an end.

"We can always come back another time." Tony smiled. "I will put the fire out and head to bed myself."

Tony kissed Amy goodnight and continued putting the fire out.

***

Halfway through the night, Tony was woken up by screams coming from Amy's room. "What the...?" He felt instantly panicked, and rushed into her room expecting the worst, only to find Amy asleep, having a nightmare.

"Amy, wake up! Are you OK?" Tony held Amy in his arms as she lay there sobbing until she fell back to sleep again.

"I am here Amy," Tony soothed.

He laid down with Amy for the rest of the night.

It was daylight and Christmas morning. Amy woke up feeling embarrassed after her nightmare. Tony was lying next to her fast asleep. She got up quietly, trying not to disturb him.

"Merry Christmas Sam," Amy whispered and gave Sam a stroke and his food.

Amy prepared the vegetables and potatoes for lunchtime then made a special breakfast for Tony.

Tony came into the kitchen rubbing his eyes.

"What time is it?"

"It is Christmas time. Did I wake you up? I was trying to be quiet," Amy hurried, trying to keep the subject on anything other than her nightmare.

"Amy, how are you feeling?"

Amy was getting red in the face not wanting to talk about it.

"I have made you a lovely breakfast of eggs, smoked salmon with avocado and a cup of your favourite coffee. Merry Christmas." Amy beamed at him, giving Tony a big kiss and hug.

"I prepared the vegetables and potatoes and gave Sam his food. All you have to do is relax and eat your breakfast."

"Thank you, Amy. And a Merry Christmas to you too."

Tony enjoyed his breakfast and went to his bedroom. A few minutes later he returned with a gift for Amy.

Amy was very excited as she unwrapped the present and opened the box.

"Tony it is gorgeous!"

"Let me help put it on."

Amy went to the mirror looking at the stunning necklace that he bought for her.

"I will treasure it forever."

Amy gave Tony his present and a little something for Sam too.

"I was not sure what to get you. I hope you like it."

Tony unwrapped his gift. It was a gold pen with his initials inscribed on it. And a mounted plaque which said: 'Whenever you are feeling blue. Know that I am right there with you.'

"Amy, I love it. They will sit proudly on my desk. Thank you." Tony hugged Amy and kissed her passionately. Sam barked waiting for his bag of treats to be opened. Amy and Tony giggled like two overgrown children.

"Amy, look," Tony said, as he beckoned her over to the window. It was snowing.

"It really is Christmas now."

They spent the rest of the day in their pyjamas. Eating and playing games.

***

It was the end of Amy and Tony's trip to the mountains. They cleaned the cabin and packed the car with their belongings.

"I am going to take Sam for a walk before the long drive home."

Amy smiled as she took one last look at the stunning mountains.

This will always be a special place that Amy would not forget.

Several hours later they arrived home. Tony took Amy's luggage into the house.

"Thank you, Tony. I had the best Christmas."

"Me too Amy, the best." He paused. "Amy, the night you woke up screaming. What happened?"

Please do not ask thought Amy.

"It was just a dream. Maybe it was to do with the meditation that day."

Tony knew that it was not the reason. *What was Amy keeping from him?*

"Well, have a brilliant time with Tara. I will call you at midnight on New Year's Eve. Make sure you answer your phone."

Tony gave Amy a lingering kiss and left.

Amy knew she had to explain to Tony about her nightmares, but would he understand?

Chapter 11

It was New Year's Eve and Tara was due home. Amy was busy getting the house ready when she heard a familiar voice behind her. Amy turned around, and there she stood.

"I'm back!"

Amy gasped. "Oh, my word, Tara you scared me! You are not due back for a few more hours yet."

"Yes, I know. I got a lift from a friend." They gave each other a big hug.

"I am so happy to see you, Tara. You go and unpack; and I will get you something to eat and drink," Amy said as she rushed to prepare something for Tara.

"It is so good to be home."

Amy poured some homemade soup into a bowl and served it with hot, home-baked crusty bread.

"It looks lovely. I have missed your cooking Amy." Tara couldn't wait to tuck in.

"So, how has the cruise been?"

"It has been amazing. We have been all around the Caribbean islands, soaking up the wonderful sunshine. When I am not singing, of course!"

Amy laughed.

"It is actually hard work. Not as glamorous as it sounds."

"You could have fooled me!" Amy said, smiling.

"So, how was your Christmas in the mountains with Tony?" Tara asked inquisitively.

"It was perfect… well, almost."

"Tell me," Tara politely insisted.

"The worst thing that could happen… I had one of my nightmares."

"What did you tell Tony?"

"That it was just a silly dream."

"And he believed you?"

"I guess so."

"Amy, I have heard your nightmares, and they are not just silly dreams. You have to tell him." Tara was starting to feel like Amy would never open up to Tony and was worried it would end the same way as it did with Luke.

"I will, but I do not want to scare him away."

"But you will if he keeps hearing you screaming and not knowing why, he will think you are some kind of nutcase!" Tara said as she started to laugh, seeing the funny side.

"That is not amusing Tara," Amy said with a straight face.

"I know Amy. Sorry. But you have to tell him."

"I will, when the moment is right."

Tara looked at Amy and shook her head.

"So, what are we going to do to see in the New Year?" asked Amy.

"I need another bowl of your delicious soup first and then I will think about it," Tara replied, as she thrusted her empty bowl in Amy's direction with a cheeky smile on her face.

***

In the evening, Amy and Tara decided to go to a pub where they knew a live band was playing. When they got there they found it bustling with people.

"Tara, Amy, come over here!" called out Simon, one of their friends. "It is so good to see you, Tara. How is it going on the cruise?"

"Fabulous, thank you."

"Are you going to give us a song later?"

"Maybe after a few drinks!" laughed Tara.

The bar was extremely busy. Everyone was having a wonderful time. There was only one hour to go before the New Year. Amy was looking forward to talking to Tony. Everyone had consumed a lot of alcohol, except Amy of course! But she was still having a good time.

"Give us a song, Tara!" someone shouted out. It was like old times, when Tara used to work there, and she was in her element up on the stage singing. There were only a few minutes to go before midnight.

"Everyone, get your drinks ready," Tara announced over the microphone. Amy was waiting for her phone call from Tony, starting to worry that it might not come.

Tara started the count down, and finally, it was one second to midnight when Amy's phone rang. She stepped outside so that she could hear better.

"Amy. Happy New Year!" Tony said happily down the phone.

"Happy New Year Tony. I miss you." Amy found herself saying.

"I am missing you too."

"When will I see you?" There was no response. "Hello? Tony? Are you still there?" Amy's phone had been cut off. *Had he hung up on her?*

Feeling disappointed, Amy turned around to go back inside the pub.

"What is that unhappy face for?" someone asked.

Amy looked up, surprised.

"Tony!" Amy exclaimed, as she ran into his arms.

"Happy New Year Amy." Tony held Amy close and gave her a very long kiss.

Amy had the biggest smile on her face.

"Wait a minute. How did you know I was here?" Amy inquired.

"A certain someone told me."

"You mean Tara?" Amy beamed. "I am so happy that she did, let's go back to my house?"

"What about Tara?" Tony asked.

"Tara will not even notice I have gone, and I doubt she will make it home tonight." Amy laughed.

***

When they got back to hers, Amy made a cup of tea for them both.

"That was such a lovely surprise. Were you supposed to be spending New Year's with your family?"

"I told them about you. They knew I wanted to be here and encouraged me to go."

"I am so happy that you are," Amy beamed. "Listen to everyone outside having a jolly time. Forget the tea, let us have a glass of elder flower wine," Amy said, feeling she'd make an exception for tonight.

Amy got two glasses from the cupboard and took the elder flower out of the refrigerator.

Tony picked up his glass and said, "Cheers to a happy, healthy, peaceful New Year. And may our relationship continue to grow stronger every day."

Tony's endearing words made Amy's heart skip a beat with joy. She was started to fall deeply for Tony, and they talked all night long, not realising the time.

"It's rather late. I had better go and let you get some sleep," Tony said casually, as he got up, preparing to leave.

Amy looked at Tony, not believing what she was about to say. "Stay the night," she said, as she took Tony by the hand and led him to her bedroom.

***

The next morning Amy woke up, almost wondering if she had imagined the amazing night she'd had, only to find Tony was still next to her with his eyes closed.

"Tony, are you awake?" she whispered.

"Yes, are you?" Tony teased as he opened his eyes and grinned at her.

Amy laughed, hitting Tony playfully.

"Are you ready for breakfast?" Amy asked.

"Do we have to get up yet? I just want to lie here with you a bit longer."

Amy snuggled closer to Tony with the biggest shy smile on her face... Amy knew he was the one. The man she could really be happy with. She felt it was time to finally tell Tony about her family. Amy closed her eyes and drifted back to sleep, feeling safe in Tony's arms.

***

Tara arrived home with a very sore head after staying out all night.

"Amy, I need you!" Tara shouted.

Amy came out of the bedroom and headed down the stairs.

"Look at the state of you Tara," Amy scolded, as she went to get some pain killers.

"Amy, never let me drink again!" Tara pleaded, feeling very sorry for herself.

"Every time you drink too much alcohol Tara, you tell me the same thing," Amy replied, almost laughing at Tara's predictability.

"Amy be kind. My head hurts," Tara moaned.

"Take these." Amy handed Tara a glass of water and two pain killers. Just then, Tony walked into the kitchen.

"Morning Tara. Did you have a good night?"

"Something like that!" Tara replied, not really paying much attention... A second later something clicked in Tara's brain and she suddenly turned around.

"Tony, did you stay here last night?" she asked, almost in disbelief. *How much had she had to drink?*

"Yes, is that a problem?"

"No, not at all, I am just a bit surprised." Tara looked at Amy with a naughty grin on her face. "Anyway, I will leave you to it. I need to go to bed. Good to see you Tony…" she said as rushed off upstairs, eager to jump under the covers and hide herself from the world for a few hours.

Amy and Tony's faces were beaming with happiness.

"I had better get myself ready and get back to take Sam out for a walk. He has probably had his legs crossed all night."

Amy burst into fits of giggles.

"Tony, can we meet later? There is something I need to talk to you about," Amy said seriously all of a sudden.

"Sure, come to my place and I will cook dinner," Tony offered, as he walked out the door. *What was it that Amy was going to tell him?* he wondered.

***

Amy was busy tidying the house, doing the washing, and vacuuming the lounge.

"Amy, please," Tara groaned whilst holding her head, gesturing to the vacuum cleaner.

"You decided to get up then?" Amy grinned, turning it off.

"What time is it?" Tara slumped down on the sofa.

"It is late, you may as well go back to bed," Amy joked. "So where did you end up last night?"

"I am not sure. Someone from the pub had a party. Anyway, lady, what did you get up to last night? Or do I need to ask?"

"What do you mean?" Amy remarked with a big smile on her face.

"Come on, tell me everything— well, not quite everything!"

"There is nothing to say, only that I have never felt like this before."

"It has been a long time Amy. No one is as happy for you as I am." Tara smiled genuinely, happy that her friend was finally opening up to someone other than just her.

"Tony is different. He makes me feel safe and I trust him. I am going to tell him everything tonight. I hope that I do not scare him off." Amy was worried about what his reaction would be.

"Tony cares about you, he will understand."

"We will see."

"Everything will be fine. Now, I need to do something to clear my head."

***

Amy arrived at Tony's feeling nervous about what she was going to say. Tony opened the door. Excitedly, Sam raced up to Amy wagging his tail and barking. "Someone's happy to see you," Tony laughed.

"Hello, Sam." Amy gave him a big hug and rubbed his head.

"I see. The dog cuddled first!" Tony teased.

"I am coming to you Mr impatient... Something smells good." Amy sniffed the air at the delicious smells coming from the kitchen.

"Why thank you, it is my new aftershave!"

"Not you," laughed Amy, "the food!"

"I hope you like Beef Wellington?" Tony asked.

"I've never had it before."

"Then you are in for a treat." Tony paused. "It is almost ready.

Make yourself at home, I will get you a drink."

Amy sat on the sofa and Sam made himself comfortable next to her.

Tony gave Amy a glass of elder flower cordial. That was her favourite drink.

"How has your day been?"

"I've just been doing the housework and making Tara's head feel worse by putting the Hoover on." They both laughed. "And how has your day been?"

"My day has been very relaxing. I took Sam for a long walk and listened to some music. I did my washing and then prepared dinner. Come and sit at the table while I serve."

"Dinner looks amazing."

"You have not tried it yet!" Tony laughed. "I am joking. I enjoy cooking, especially when it is for a gorgeous lady."

Amy took a bite of the beef Wellington.

"It tastes delicious Tony; where did you learn to cook like that?" Amy asked, surprised.

"My mum is an amazing cook. I learned everything from her."

"I will have to get a few cooking tips."

"My mum would be delighted if you did ask. There is lemon cheesecake afterwards. I bought it from the shop though." Tony grinned.

After they had finished dinner and the cheesecake, Amy got up to wash the plates.

"Amy leave it. Go put your feet up and relax. I will make coffee."

Once they had both had their coffee, Amy decided it was time. It was now or never.

"Tony, there is something you need to know. I feel very uncomfortable about this, so please be patient with me."

Tony took Amy by the hand. "It's okay, just take your time."

Amy took in a deep breath as she mustered up the courage to say what she needed to say. "The reason I have never spoken about my family has always been because it is too painful. I grew up in a very unsettled home. My dad was an abusive alcoholic and a gambling man. Mum was an incredible lady. My brother, Josh, was my hero and best friend. There was always a distressing atmosphere when Dad was around. He was normally drunk most of the time. Dad would say the vilest things to Mum and would hit her. The screams were so frightening."

Amy stopped to take another breath. Tony gave Amy a reassuring squeeze of her hand.

Amy continued, "Dad was never violent towards me and Josh until that harrowing night. Tony, it was horrible, walking into the kitchen and seeing the blood everywhere. I am sorry, I cannot talk about it anymore."

Amy wiped the tears off her face and Tony held her tight.

"You have nothing to be sorry for. When we were in the mountains, the dream was about what happened?"

"Yes, I have had really terrible nightmares and so much heartache ever since. It will not go away."

"Amy, you have been carrying this around for all these years. Have you ever thought about getting help?"

"I have tried. When I find the courage, I clam up and cannot go through with it."

"Have you spoken to Tara about it?"

"Yes, Tara is the only one who knows everything, except my foster parents who are no longer alive. Tara has been my rock and is very supportive." Amy felt very appreciative that she had Tara as a friend.

"So, you have kept it to yourself all this time?" Tony asked.

"Yes. I just need you to understand that when I have these nightmares, I am not some crazy person."

"Of course you are not crazy Amy. Thank you for trusting me, it could not have been easy to tell me." Tony paused in thought. "We will get you the help required and get you through this, I promise," Tony said, as he pulled Amy close to him and looked into her eyes. "I love you."

Amy looked at Tony as tears of relief and happiness started to fall down her face. "I love you too."

They sat there for a few moments snuggling. Amy suddenly felt drained.

"Can I stay here with you tonight?"

"Stay as long as you wish. It has been a long night; you look exhausted. Go to bed and I will be in soon."

Amy made her way to bed whilst Tony stayed up pondering for a while. *How can I get the best help for Amy?* he thought.

After a while, he stroked Sam on the head, switched off the lights and joined Amy in bed.

Halfway through the night, Tony could feel Amy tossing and turning a lot and speaking in her sleep. Then she started to scream.

"Amy, wake up," he said, as he gently tugged at her shoulder. "I'm here."

Amy woke up sweating. "I'm so sorry, Tony."

Tony got up and brought her some water.

"Is it always the same dream?" Tony asked.

"Mostly. All I see is Mum and Josh covered in blood, holding their hands out for my help, but I cannot reach them. Dad is standing in the background with a drink in his hand, laughing."

"Amy, I am here for you. You will not go through this alone," Tony said, as he cradled her back to sleep.

***

When Amy woke up the next morning, she was in bed alone. *I knew it. Tony thinks I am crazy,* she thought.

Tony brought Amy in a cup of tea.

"How are you feeling?" he asked, passing her the mug.

Amy was so happy and relieved to see Tony.

"I am fine. How come you are up so early?"

"I've started looking for a councillor." Tony had already found a couple of possibilities.

He really does care, Amy thought.

"Did you have any luck?" she asked.

"I found a few, but I am not sure they are right for you. I will keep looking… You will beat this, Amy."

Finally, Amy was able to talk about that dreadful evening. She still had a long way to go, but, with Tony and Tara by her side, she could see a light at the end of the rainbow.

Chapter 12

Amy and Tony's relationship was growing stronger every day, and so were Amy's nightmares.

"Tara, I do not understand. Since I have told Tony about my nightmares, they have been getting worse and becoming more frequent."

"Are you any closer to finding someone to help?"

"We have approached a few counsellors, but not the right ones. Tony is still looking."

"Amy, a friend of mine may be able to help you. Her name is Mary Beth. She is more of a spiritual healer than a councillor."

"You know a spiritual healer?" Amy giggled. "The only spirits you know come in a bottle!"

"Very droll Amy," Tara said, straight faced. "Seriously, she has helped a lot of people overcome emotional challenges. Go and see her?"

"I'm not sure about that Tara."

"What have you got to lose? Talk it through with Tony, see what he thinks."

"He will be here very soon. I'll run it by him."

As Amy spoke, there was a knock at the door. Tara let Tony in.

"Hi Tara, how are you?"

"I'm very good, thank you. I was just saying to Amy that I know a spiritual healer who may be able to help her."

"You know a spiritual healer? I thought the only—"

Tara interrupted, "Yes Tony, Amy has already done that one!"

Amy and Tony laughed.

"What do you think Amy? Is it something you want to look into?"

"I have to give it a try. Will you come with me?"

"I told you, I will support you all the way. Of course I will come with you."

"Perfect, I will arrange an appointment for you," Tara said.

Tara left Amy and Tony together whilst she called Mary Beth.

***

The following week, Amy had an appointment to see Mary Beth. Tony went with her for moral support.

"I am not sure if I can do this." Amy anxiously paced up and down.

"It is only a chat, and I will be with you," Tony reassured Amy.

Amy nervously knocked on the door.

Mary Beth answered. "Hello, you must be Amy. Come in."

"This is my partner, Tony."

Mary Beth shook his hand. "It is good to meet you both. Please, take a seat. Tara mentioned briefly that you are having issues with nightmares."

Amy nodded feeling very uncomfortable... Tony gently squeezed Amy's hand.

"This first session is just to get to know each other and what you want to achieve from the sessions," Mary Beth started. "Some people think that spiritual healers are a bit weird and freaky, right?"

Mary Beth smiled. "I do not give magic potions or anything like that. I simply connect through divine energy, the breath of life, that links me to a greater source. You may refer to it as the Universe, God, Angels, Buddha, or whoever you believe in. Working on a deep level of our spiritual being, helps to release what no longer serves us. My purpose is to guide others on their healing journey and to help them to free themselves."

Amy looked at Tony, confused.

"How does this work?" Tony inquired intriguingly.

"With energy healing, I always start with meditation to help you relax. I invite my spirit guides to keep us grounded and shielded throughout the session."

"What do you mean by grounded and shielded?"

"Grounding balances our energy field mentally and physically, draining away negative energy from entering that space. Some people like to find a quiet environment outside in nature, visualizing, or chanting, connecting with the mother earth. But this is mostly performed inside during a session.

"Through energy, we gather from the world around us toxicity. By shielding ourselves using divine light, we create a personal shield of protection from darkness."

Tony was taking in much more than Amy.

"Amy, you can either stay seated or lie on my therapy couch, whichever makes you more comfortable. I then gently position my hands on or above your clothed body, scanning for blocked areas, reducing any stress, encouraging a healthy flow of energy, and helping you to feel relaxed. Through this procedure, you may get emotional, have visions, see colours, or just fall asleep. This is all perfectly normal. When the session has ended, we will talk about what you experienced and how it made you feel. Does that all make sense? Are there any questions?"

"How long will it take for Amy to see any results?"

"That I cannot tell you. Healing takes time. Amy, you have taken the first steps by coming to see me and acknowledge that you require some assistance. We shall take each session at a time, and I will give you guidance so that you can practice by yourself at home." Mary Beth paused. "Amy, you have been very quiet. Is there anything that you want to ask or are concerned about?"

Amy felt awkward. "How many sessions will I need to have?"

"That all depends on how deep the healing has to go, and your response to releasing the feelings and emotions. The pain and heartache have been with you for a number of years. It will take time. Would you like to go ahead?"

Amy looked at Tony for the answer.

"Amy, do what is right for you. You need to move forward. This could be the start of a whole new chapter. I will support you in whatever you decide."

Amy turned to Mary Beth. "I want my life back. Can you really help me?" Amy still felt unsure, but was willing to give it a try.

"Amy, yes, I can help you. All that I ask is that you come to each session with an open heart. The healing is within you. I am just a vessel to help guide the flow of energy through your body releasing undesired emotions."

"Yes, I would like that very much."

"I want to get you started as soon as possible. Are you available tomorrow?"

"I can come straight after work."

"That would be perfect."

"Thank you, Mary Beth."

Tony put his arm around Amy and smiled. "It is going to be Ok Amy."

Amy was very quiet on the way home feeling nervous about the next session. When she got home, Tara was eager to find out how the session had gone.

"How did it go with Mary Beth?" Tara asked.

"Tara, it was quite overwhelming... Tony seems to process the information better than me. I just sat there not saying a word."

"Amy, you did really well. It was a lot to take in. I found Mary Beth fascinating. It sounded very positive."

"Thank you for coming with me Tony. I could not have done it without you."

"I will always be here for you Amy… I must go now. I will leave you ladies to talk."

Amy walked Tony to the door.

"I will pick you up after work tomorrow."

"Thank you. I love you Tony."

"I love you too Amy. See you tomorrow." Tony gave Amy a kiss goodbye and left. Amy closed the door, turning back to her conversation with Tara.

"How do you feel about seeing Mary Beth for your first healing session?"

"To be honest, Tara, I am terrified."

"You have no need to worry about it, Amy. Mary Beth will take good care of you."

"I have no doubt that she will. I am just terrified of reliving it all."

"But that is the idea Amy, so that you can finally let it go and live the life you should be. Free from all the stress and anxiety this has caused you."

"I know you are right, Tara, and I have to do this, but it will not be easy. Anyway, I am going to shower and go to bed. See you in the morning. Love you," Amy said, as she started to make her way to the bathroom.

"Love you too," Tara called back at her.

***

The next morning at work, Amy was feeling quite anxious thinking about her session later that day with Mary Beth.

"Amy are you OK? You seem to be in a world of your own," Gill asked.

"I have a slight headache but I will be fine, thank you for asking."

Amy ploughed into her work, anything to keep her mind occupied.

At the end of the day, Tony was waiting to take Amy to see Mary Beth.

"How are you feeling?"

"I am feeling anxious and nervous."

"That is to be expected. You can do this Amy," Tony said encouragingly.

They left Amy's work and soon arrived at Mary Beth's.

"Hello, it is good to see you again," Mary Beth greeted them with a warm smile on her face.

"What is that lovely smell?" Amy asked.

"That is my lavender essential oil. It helps to create calmness and peace."

The room felt very peaceful. A candle was burning whilst gentle, relaxing music played quietly in the background.

"Please, have a seat. Before we start, can you explain a little about the cause of these nightmares and what events took place when they started?"

Amy looked at Tony for reassurance. He gave her a little wink.

Amy was feeling nervous, not wanting to relive that night, but knew she needed to. She started by telling Mary Beth about her childhood, growing up in an unsettled home, and she spoke with love and fond memories of her Mum and brother Josh. Amy was finding it difficult to continue and Mary Beth picked up on this, deciding not to push her too much too soon.

"OK, we will leave it there for now and proceed with meditation. Are you ready Amy?" Mary Beth asked.

"No. Not really." Amy did not feel confident.

"If at any point you want to stop, just say. There is no pressure, we will take it slowly and at your pace. Make yourself comfortable and close your eyes. We will start by focusing on our breathing. Take a gentle deep breath in and exhale slowly through the mouth. Repeat two more times.

"This meditation and energy healing is with good intention, helping Amy on her journey towards inner peace and freedom, to release what no longer serves her. I ask our spirit guides to shield us with divine light, releasing all negative energies. And so, it is."

There was a short pause and Mary Beth continued, "Now, take a deep breath in and release it and when you are ready… now open your eyes. Amy, how do you feel?"

"I still have that anxious feeling in my stomach..."

"Now we will go through the energy healing. Would you like to stay seated where you are, or lay down on the couch?"

"Stay where I am?"

"Yes, of course. Tony, can I ask you to sit on the other chair, so that I have space to move around Amy? Amy, remember, we can stop at any time. I will chime my Tingsha bells at the beginning to promote the flow of healthy energy through the body and then again at the end. When you are ready, close your eyes, take a deep breath, and release it."

Tony watched with interest, absorbing the energy, and feeling very relaxed.

Mary Beth began by laying her hands on the top of Amy's head and slowly continued moving down to each of the chakras. There seemed to be a lot of blockages that needed to be cleared.

Amy was starting to get a bit agitated and started coughing. Amy opened her eyes.

"Can we stop now?"

Mary Beth chimed her bells, gave Amy a glass of water and sat down opposite her. Tony re-joined Amy on the sofa, taking hold of her hand.

"How do you feel Amy?"

"Like I want to be sick. I kept feeling this thick sticky tar in my throat. It was horrible."

"That makes a lot of sense, let me explain. There are seven chakras in our bodies that can sometimes get blocked when we experience too much stress and anxiety. The reason you had that feeling in your throat is because for years you have been afraid to communicate and express your feelings. When we spoke earlier, you told me of the unsettled home life that you had. Do you think you can tell me a bit more?"

"Maybe next time. I've had enough for today."

"I completely understand. You did really well, Amy." Mary Beth was pleased with the progress they had made that session, and was confident she could help Amy.

"Can I ask a question?" Tony asked.

"Of course you can, what is it?"

"What are chakras?"

"Sorry, I should have explained. Chakras, or spinning wheels, supply energy along the spinal column to particular parts of the body." Mary Beth stands and points to each chakra. "The crown, third eye, throat, heart, solar plexus, sacral, and root. When any of these are blocked and not aligned, the flow of energy stops them from functioning at their best, causing stress, anxiety, even trauma, whether that be mentally, physically, or emotionally." Mary Beth continued, "My job is to help the energy flow back into alignment and balance the chakras, but the healing starts from within you Amy."

"Thank you for explaining that to me," Tony replied.

"Amy, I would like to see you again in two days. Have plenty of water tonight. You may feel tired, have a headache or even be emotional. These are normal, so do not worry, just rest."

Amy and Tony left and made their way back to Amy's. On the journey home, they started to discuss the events of the session.

"I found that enlightening, how are you feeling about it Amy?"

"It's early days, Tony. I will tell you after a few more sessions. I just feel exhausted and need to go to bed," Amy said sleepily.

Tony dropped Amy home.

"I will call you tomorrow," Tony told Amy.

"Thank you again Tony for supporting me. I am really very grateful." Amy smiled and kissed Tony on the cheek.

"Always Amy. Have a good night's sleep. I love you," he said, as he walked off.

Amy went straight to her bedroom and fell onto the bed, too tired to even get undressed.

Chapter 13

Amy was extremely busy at work dealing with new contracts that she'd had no time to think about the next session with Mary Beth...

Tony called her just before she was about to leave. "Amy, I am so sorry, I have to attend an emergency meeting. Will you be OK to go by yourself this evening?"

"That is fine, I will have to go on my own at some point. I will speak to you later. Love you," she said and hung up.

After a short drive there Amy arrived at Mary Beth's with a sick feeling in her stomach.

Come on Amy, pull yourself together. Just knock on the door, she thought.

After finally mustering up the courage Amy knocked, and Mary Beth answered the door.

"Amy, please, come in. Tony is not with you this evening?" she questioned.

"He had an emergency meeting at work that he could not get out of. So, it is just me!"

"How were you after our last session?"

"Exhausted. I was so tired I fell asleep with my clothes on." Amy gave a slight grin.

"This evening we will do the same as before. Starting with meditation and then the energy healing."

"May I lay on the couch this time?"

"Of course you can. Let us do it all from the couch. Are you OK with that?"

"Yes, that's fine."

"If you want to get onto the couch and make yourself comfortable. I will put a blanket over you if you feel cold. When you are ready, close your eyes and take a deep breath in and slowly release it again."

Mary Beth went through the meditation with Amy and then began with the healing. Whilst Mary Beth was working on the chakras, she could see that Amy was getting distressed, throwing her head from side to side. All of a sudden Amy sprung up, with floods of tears streaming down her face.

"Amy, you are safe." Mary Beth held Amy in her arms. She took a few deep breaths and calmed down. Mary Beth got her a glass of water.

"Amy let us sit on the sofa. Are you OK?"

Amy nodded her head, unable to speak for a few minutes.

"Can you tell me what was making you so distressed?"

"I must have fallen asleep. I had one of my nightmares."

"What happened in your nightmare?"

"The same thing that always happens. Mum and Josh are covered in blood holding their hands out, but I cannot reach them. Dad is standing behind them laughing," Amy said sadly, suddenly feeling like she wanted to cry again.

"Thank you for sharing and trusting me with this Amy."

"Mary Beth, I do not understand why the nightmares have got worse since I told Tony. They are happening most nights now." The stress and lack of sleep was starting to impact Amy's ability to function properly.

"Amy, it has been many years since you have shared what

happened. You have trust in the people that you have told, which is a big step and part of you letting go, even though you may not think it is. There is a long way to go still, but I do know that you will get through this. Let me ask, how do you find meditation?"

"I do find that it relaxes me."

"That is good to know." Mary Beth handed Amy two CD's. "Listen to these guided meditation and relaxation music CDs when you are feeling anxious and tense. You can even listen to them and meditate together with Tony and Tara."

Amy laughed.

"No offense, but Tara is not the kind of person to sit and meditate. But I think Tony will enjoy it."

"I will book you for two more sessions next week. If you have any questions in the meantime, call me. Amy, you are doing well. Enjoy the weekend and I will see you soon."

Amy called Tony as soon as she left.

"How did it go?"

"It was fine to start with but I fell asleep during the meditation and had a nightmare... It was horrible," Amy cried.

"In a way, it was probably a good thing. Mary Beth got to see how you are when you have these nightmares."

"I guess so. She gave me some CDs of relaxation music and meditations. She suggested that maybe we could do them together sometimes."

"I would be up for that. I like meditation. When are you seeing her again?"

"Mary Beth has booked me in for two sessions next week."

"That is good. We will have a chilled-out weekend at my house and listen to the CD's. What do you think?"

"I think that sound's perfect."

"I will see you tomorrow. Love you, Amy."

"Love you too," Amy said and hung up.

When she got home, Amy called out to Tara, "I'm back."

Tara came down from the bathroom.

"How did your session go?" she asked.

"It could have been better… I had one of my nightmares."

"You had a nightmare? Do you have them when you are awake now?" Tara could not help herself.

"Tara you can be so annoying sometimes."

"Amy I was joking!" She laughed.

"Mary Beth gave me these two CDs to listen to. Relaxing music and meditation. She even suggested that you may want to join me... Now, that *was* amusing." Amy smiled.

"I agree. It is amusing!"

They both roared with laughter.

"What are your plans for the weekend?"

"I am staying over at Tony's place, so you have the house to yourself."

"Party time!" Tara said excitedly as she watched Amy's unamused expression. "I'm only teasing you Amy."

"I am glad to hear it."

"Would you like a cup of tea?"

"No, thank you. I am going to listen to my music," Amy said, as she gestured to her CDs.

"Enjoy… I'll make plans for my party." Tara was in one of her teasing moods, and gave Amy a big cheeky smile.

Amy put her pyjamas on and made herself comfortable, got into bed and played the relaxing music, sending Amy off into a deep sleep. Right through until the following morning.

***

Amy woke up bright and breezy after having the best night's sleep. She went down to the kitchen, switched the radio on and made coffee whilst dancing and singing.

"Amy, you are chirpy this morning. Actually, why are you so happy?" Tara asked, rubbing her eyes.

"I had the most restful sleep Tara, the music certainly worked."

"Well, if it makes you feel like this in the morning, I suggest you listen to it every night!" Tara yawned.

"I may just do that." Amy twirled around, nearly falling over.

Tara could not help but laugh.

"I have chores to do and then pack for my stay over at Tony's. What are you going to do with yourself? And, before you say it, no party!" Amy said in a stern voice, but with a playful expression on her face.

"Amy, what do you take me for?" Tara rolled her eyes jokingly.

"I am not going to answer that," Amy replied as she playfully threw a tea towel at Tara. "You can dry the dishes."

"What dishes?" Tara looked around at the tidy kitchen. Amy had already left the room.

***

It was mid-afternoon by the time Amy had finished all of her chores. Then Tony arrived.

"Hello gorgeous lady, how are you?" Tony asked in an alluring voice.

"I am feeling on top of the world!" Amy said, as she gave Tony a big hug, spinning him around.

"And why is that?" Tony beamed.

"I had the best sleep. It was due to the relaxing music. I have not slept that well in a very long time."

"I could do with some of that." Tony winked.

"Do not worry, I am bringing them both with me."

Tony put his arms around Amy's waist.

"I have a surprise for you."

"I love surprises, what is it?" Amy clapped her hands together with excitement.

"Well, how would you like an afternoon of pampering?"

Amy's eyes light up.

"I have booked a fabulous spa day for us both at the Avalon hotel."

"Tony, that is one of the most exclusive Spa rooms in town."

"Remember the meeting I had yesterday?"

"Yes, I do."

"It just happened to be the owner of the Avalon. He has given us free range of the spa. Not only that, but a room in the hotel for the night."

"Tony, that is incredible. I had better repack my bag!"

Amy rushed by Tara on her way up the stairs.

"What is Amy so excited about?" Tara asked.

"We are going to the spa at the Avalon hotel and staying the night."

"No wonder she is happy." She laughed. "Tony, how is Amy getting on with her sessions?"

"Why do you ask?"

"I am just checking. I want the best for Amy."

"It is still early days, I want the best for her too. Mary Beth seems to know what she is doing."

Just as Tara was about to respond Amy bounded into the room like an excited puppy. "I am ready. Shall we go?" she asked. Tony smiled and started to walk with her to the door.

"Have an amazing time you two," Tara said as they were about to leave.

Amy paused. "Tara–"

"Yes Amy, I know, no party!" Tara chuckled. "Now go on, get out of here!"

***

They arrived at the hotel and it was just as fancy as Amy had imagined. "Tony, this place is amazing! I feel like royalty."

Amy was taking in every detail of the Avalon hotel lobby.

"Well, you are my princess," smiled Tony.

After checking in at the reception, Amy and Tony entered the glass lift that took them to floor number twenty-two, where their room was. Amy could not believe the size of the room.

"Tony, you could fit half of my house in here. And look at that view, we can pretend to be prince and princess for the day." Amy giggled.

"Would Her Highness like to go for some relaxing pampering?" Tony asked, bowing playfully.

"Why yes, my prince, that would be delightful," Amy said in the poshest voice she could muster.

Amy and Tony were in fits of laughter as they headed down to the spa rooms.

When they went into the spa room they were greeted by Magda, the receptionist.

"Welcome to Avalon Spa. Is this your first visit with us?"

Amy and Tony both nodded.

Magda led them to a room.

"This is your private section for the day. You have luxury robes and slippers to be worn in the spa area. A mini cooler which has water and soft drinks, and a shower room with towels. There are many treatments available and no need to book any of them. You may use the swimming pool and sauna. If there is anything else you require, I will be here. Enjoy your time at the Avalon Spa."

Amy and Tony spent the rest of the afternoon and early evening at the spa having as many treatments as they could. Amy even had her nails manicured and painted.

After the most relaxing day at the spa, Amy and Tony got ready back in their room to go down to the hotel's restaurant.

The restaurant hotel maître welcomed and showed them to their table.

"Tony, look at all this different cutlery. What ones are you supposed to use?"

"I have no idea. Just pretend we know what we are doing."

They both giggled quietly.

The waiter came and took their order. They had a starter, main, and desert. Feeling very full, Amy and Tony headed up to their room very relaxed and tired.

"Tony thank you so much for the best day."

"No need to thank me. Charles gave us this amazing day. I am happy that you have had a good time Amy."

Exhausted and content, they fell asleep instantly.

At some point during the night, Amy started becoming distressed and restless, disturbing Tony's sleep. Aware of the signs, he knew that Amy was going into a nightmare, so he gently woke her up. Amy stirred and then fell back to sleep.

***

The next morning Amy was feeling happy. Laying there looking at Tony sleeping, thinking how lucky she was to have him... Tony's eyes started to open.

"Morning my handsome prince. How did you sleep?" She smiled at him lovingly.

Tony rolled over and cuddled Amy and told her what had happened in the night. Amy got out of bed feeling guilty.

"I am so sorry Tony. We had such a lovely day and then I went and spoiled it."

"Amy, you have not spoiled anything. You never had a nightmare."

"Only because you could see what was coming. You are not always going to be there to stop them from happening."

Tony got out of bed and held Amy.

"Amy. Everything is fine."

"That's just it Tony. It is not fine, far from it."

***

Amy and Tony went for a late breakfast in the hotel restaurant before heading home.

"I am sorry Tony for being miserable this morning. I just want the nightmares to end."

"Amy, you have no need to apologise. You did not have a nightmare. That is a good thing."

"I know it is Tony, but you cannot be there every time to wake me up before one is about to happen."

"Amy, you are being too hard on yourself. Listen, we had an amazing time being pampered in our palace."

Amy smiled.

"Let us just focus on that and take it one day at a time. OK?"

"OK, my prince. Maybe Mary Beth can work some of her positive energy on me tomorrow."

"Remember, one day at a time. You will get there Amy. I promise."

***

The next day Amy arrived at Mary Beth's.

"Amy, lovely to see you again. Please have a seat. Did you have a good weekend?"

"Yes, thank you. Tony and I went for the night to a very posh and exclusive hotel and had the most amazing spa treatments."

"Now, that sounds glorious. What a treat." Mary Beth sighed dreamily.

"It was. We pretended to be a prince and princess. It was so much fun."

"I am happy that you had a good time, but I can sense it was not all fun. What happened?"

"What do you think?" Amy frowned.

"You had a nightmare?"

"Well, I was on the verge of having one, Tony woke me up before it escalated. Mary Beth, I cannot keep doing this to Tony."

"Amy, you need to open up and talk to me. Do you think you can?"

"I will try my best," Amy conceded.

"First, we will go through meditation and then healing. Is that OK with you?" Mary Beth asked.

Amy nodded and laid on the couch. Mary Beth continued with the meditation. Amy could feel herself drifting into a sense of peace and calm. The healing was going well, then Amy started to get distressed. Sitting up quickly, Amy could not continue. Getting up from the couch, she went and sat on the chair.

"Are you Ok? Take a minute and gather yourself together."

"I am fine. It was the same old thing. Mary Beth, I want it to stop!"

"It will stop Amy. Are you ready to talk?"

Amy nodded her head in agreement.

"Shall we start at the beginning? Tell me what your relationship was like with your parents and your brother."

"Mum was so gentle and loving, always smelling like roses. It was comforting for me. Dad was an angry, gambling drunk. Any little thing would set him off. Josh was my best friend. He protected me from everything; we were always together. Josh worked hard so that he could save enough money and take me and Mum away from Dad to be safe."

"What do you mean by safe?"

"Safe so that Mum would be free from Dad's violent abusive behaviour. He said the most vile, cruel things and would hit her. Mum would always give him the benefit of the doubt. She lived in the hope that one day he would change, but it never did."

"Were you ever scared that your father would hurt you and Josh?"

"No, not that he would abuse us physically, but it did have an effect on us mentally, especially me."

"What do you mean?"

"Mum and Dad would argue all the time. Listening to her screams when he hit her, and there was nothing I could do to help."

"And what about Josh. Did he do something to try to help your Mum?"

Amy went quiet.

"I do not want to talk about it anymore."

"OK, Amy. We can you stop if that is what you want to do?"

"I want to carry on. I just cannot say the words."

Mary Beth got up from the chair.

"Amy, may I do some more healing for you? I want to concentrate on your throat chakra."

Amy agreed and closed her eyes.

Mary Beth stood behind Amy and placed her hands slightly away from her throat area and continued. At the end of the healing, Amy opened her eyes feeling relaxed. Whilst they were discussing the treatment, Amy started coughing uncontrollably, finding it difficult to catch her breath.

"Amy breathe, focus on me. Take a deep breath and slowly release it." She paused. "And again."

Amy continued with the breathing exercises until she calmed down and the coughing stopped. Mary Beth got her some water.

"That was a powerful release from you Amy. How are you feeling?"

"What just happened?"

"That was your throat chakra opening, clearing the way for you to speak your truth about what's causing your nightmares. I know it seems a bit frightening, but it is a good thing. I would like to continue tomorrow if that is OK with you?"

"Yes, that will be fine. Mary Beth, do you think I can do this?"

"I most certainly do Amy."

Amy decided to call Tony to come and pick her up as she was feeling a bit shaky after the session. He took her back home.

"Hey, how did it go? Amy, you look worn out." Tara was just making coffee.

"It was an intense energy release." Amy explained what had occurred.

"That sounds like powerful stuff Amy. Were you able to talk about that night?"

"No, I was doing so well, but I just could not get the words out. It was scary. Mary Beth said it was my throat chakra opening. I am going back tomorrow."

"That sounds positive."

"Amy, this is the longest session that you've had. There is definitely progress, you are doing really well." Tony put his arms around Amy and gently kissed her.

"Get a room, you two," Tara interrupted, making light of the conversation.

"I am feeling tired, I must go to bed. Tony, would you like to stay?"

"I had better get home. I still have a lot of work to do. Do you want me to come with you tomorrow?"

"I have to do this by myself."

"Ok. But call me when you have finished. Be good Tara." Tony waved.

"I am always good! Night handsome."

Amy rolled her eyes, smiled, and walked Tony to the door.

"Sleep well gorgeous, I will speak with you tomorrow. Love you."

"Love you too."

Amy walked back into the kitchen.

"I am so proud of you, Amy. I know how difficult this has been for you."

"Thank you, Tara, for being there for me."

"What are best friends for?"

Tara gave Amy the biggest hug before going to bed.

***

The following day Amy got up early to get ready to go and see Mary Beth. Thinking about yesterday's session, Amy was feeling stronger, and was able to focus more positively. After a cup of calming herbal tea, Amy left the house.

Amy arrived at Mary Beth's confidently knocking on the door.

"Amy, welcome. Please come and have a seat. How are you feeling after yesterday?"

"I felt drained, to be honest, but today I woke up feeling more positive."

"I am glad to hear that Amy. Do you think you can continue from yesterday's conversation?"

"I am going to try my best."

"Let us get into position and begin our session."

Amy always enjoyed going through meditation first. It was relaxing, helping to put her in a good space before the healing.

Mary Beth could feel that there was more flow with the energies around Amy's chakras, but there were still some blockages in the throat and heart areas. The healing session went calmly and ended smoothly.

"Amy, tell me more about Josh?"

"Josh was hilarious, he always made me laugh. He took care of me, he was a big brother and Dad all rolled into one. Josh was just like Mum, kind and caring. I miss him so much."

"Josh sounds like a wonderful person."

"He truly was Mary Beth."

"Now, do you think you can tell me the reason for the nightmares?

Amy felt a shudder go through her. She took a few deep breaths and started to share with Mary Beth.

"As I have already told you. Dad was violent and abusive towards Mum. When Dad lost his job, of course, he took it out on her. On that night, the arguing and shouting was worse than before. Dad was hitting Mum a lot; you could tell by her screams. I hid under the bed covers to drown out the sounds whilst Josh went to get help. The noise suddenly stopped. I came out from under the covers and slowly opened the door. It was very quiet as I went down the stairs."

Amy stopped as tears streamed down her face.

"You are doing so well Amy." Mary Beth held Amy's hand.

"I got to the bottom of the stairs and walked towards the kitchen. The light was shining through the gap in the door. I pushed the door open and went in. Broken glass was everywhere. The table and chairs were turned upside down. I could not see anyone. Walking into the room a bit further I saw Mum and Dad. It was horrific. I had never seen so much blood. There was a large piece of glass that had gone right through my Mum. They were both dead. I heard a whimper from the corner of the room. Josh laid in a pool of blood, it pouring from his head. I bent down. 'Josh, I am going to help you' I told him. He opened his eyes for a second and whispered 'sorry', and then he died..." Amy sobbed so hard. "Mary Beth, there was nothing I could do to save him!"

Mary Beth cradled Amy in her arms with a tear in her eye as felt Amy's pain.

When Amy had calmed down, she apologised to Mary Beth.

"Amy there is no need to apologise. That was an incredible breakthrough! How do you feel?"

"Relieved, I did it. After all these years, I was able to speak about it. I cannot thank you enough. Do you think the nightmares will end now?"

"We have not quite finished yet, Amy. Even though you have made amazing progress, there is still one more thing to do that will complete your healing."

Amy looked at Mary Beth puzzled.

"You have to open your heart to forgiveness."

"I do not understand."

"Amy, you need to be able to forgive your father."

"Are you kidding me Mary Beth? That man took everything away that I had, and you expect me to forgive him?"

Amy was getting angry. *How could she even ask that of her? After everything he had done.*

"Amy, forgiving is part of letting go, so that you can move forward and free yourself from that prison that has kept you locked up all these years. Forgiveness does not mean that what your Dad did was right or that you must forget. But there are choices about how we wish to live, and only you can decide that. You have worked so hard Amy, do not throw that away by holding on to hatred. Take back control of your life. Be happy and at peace. You deserve it."

"Never will I forgive him, Mary Beth. Do you understand? Never!"

Amy was beside herself with rage as she stormed off out of Mary Beth's, slamming the door on the way out.

As soon as Amy got home she threw herself on the sofa and sobbed her heart out.

"I will never forgive him!" she kept repeating to herself.

The doorbell rang but Amy ignored it.

"Amy, open the door. It is me, Tony."

"Not now, Tony!" Amy shouted. "I will call you later."

"Amy, I am not leaving. Open this door."

Amy let Tony in and fell into his arms, sobbing.

After a while, Amy calmed down and Tony made her a cup of tea.

"How did you know I was here?" Amy asked as she dried her eyes.

"Mary Beth called me. She was really concerned about you. What happened?"

Amy explained what went on in the session.

"Mary Beth expects me to forgive that man, but how can I? He killed my family."

"Mary Beth is trying to help you and she is right. It is time to let go, and if that means forgiving your dad and moving on, then—"

"How dare you? Who are you to tell me what I should be doing?" Amy interrupted Tony.

Tony had never seen Amy so angry.

"Amy, I am not telling you anything. Mary Beth and I just want to help. Do not let him destroy you as well!"

"Tony just go! Leave. I want to be by myself."

"Amy I am not leaving you on your own in this state."

"I said, GO!" Amy shouted.

Tony gave in, and walked to the door to leave. "I will call you later," Tony said as he left, bumping into Tara on the way out.

"Amy what is going on? Tony looked so upset."

"Tara, it was all going so well."

Amy broke down in tears again. Tara sat comforting her throughout the day.

***

Later that evening, Amy had calmed down, ready to talk with Tara.

"Are you feeling better?"

"Yes, thank you. It has been an emotional day. I feel so guilty about speaking to Tony and Mary Beth in such a rude way. I know that they are only trying to help."

"Why were you so angry?" Tara asked.

"The session with Mary Beth went really well. I was able to talk about that night. It was such a relief."

"So, what went wrong?"

"Mary Beth asked me to open my heart and forgive my dad. I went mad at her for even suggesting it. I will never do that Tara."

"Mary Beth would never ask you to do something that was not good for your wellbeing. And why were you angry with Tony?"

"Because he agreed with her."

"Oh, Amy. Tony loves you so very much, he only wants what is best for you."

"Tara, I know. I just cannot agree with him and Mary Beth. They were not there that night. I will not forgive my father. But I will apologise to them both tomorrow."

***

At the end of Amy's workday, she phoned Mary Beth.

"Hello Mary Beth, it is Amy."

"Amy, how are you?"

"I am good, thank you. I want to apologise for my outburst yesterday. I should not have spoken to you in that way. I found the session quite overwhelming."

"Amy, your reaction was very normal. There is no need to apologise. Your progress has been amazing. Will you come and see me after the weekend? There is something I want to suggest."

"Yes, I will be there. See you then."

Now it was time to phone Tony.

"Tony it is me."

"Hello gorgeous. I am so sorry Amy that I upset you."

"Tony, I am the one who has to apologise. Yesterday was overwhelming for me and I took my frustration out on you. Can you forgive me?"

"There is nothing to forgive. I love you Amy."

"And I love you too, Tony. I phoned Mary Beth. I am going to see her after the weekend."

"Talking about the weekend. How would you feel about meeting my parents? They are sort of expecting us for lunch on Saturday."

"That would be lovely, I look forward to meeting them." Amy paused. "Tony are we OK?"

"Yes, absolutely. I will pick you up on Saturday."

"Thank you Tony, for being so understanding."

"I will always be there supporting you Amy. See you Saturday. Love you."

"Love you too."

Chapter 14

Saturday arrived and Amy was busy getting ready to meet Tony's parents.

"Amy do you fancy a girl's day out shopping and having lunch?" Tara asked.

"Sorry Tara not today. I am going to meet Tony's parents, he will be here soon."

"Meeting the parents? Things must be serious," Tara teased Amy.

"They must be." Amy smiled shyly.

"Remember I am going back on the cruise next weekend. It will be good to spend a day together before then, just the two of us."

"Tara, I forgot. It has come around so quickly. I will take Friday off of work, and we can have that girly day then."

"I will hold you to that," Tara replied as the doorbell rang.

"Tony is here. How do I look?"

"Amy, you look lovely. Stop panicking and have a good day."

Amy opened the door. There were an army of butterflies fluttering around Amy's stomach, nervous about meeting Tony's parents.

"You look as gorgeous as ever." Tony kissed Amy.

"Do I have everything? Flowers, chocolates, elder flower wine…" Amy fretted, as she tried to think if there was anything she had missed.

"The kitchen sink?" Tony laughed at Amy.

"Stop teasing me. I am really nervous."

"There is no need to be. My parents will love you."

***

It took about an hour to get to his parents.

"We are here." Tony beeped the car horn.

"I feel sick." Amy was feeling really anxious.

"Everything will be fine." Tony leaned over and gave Amy a reassuring peck on the cheek.

Tony's parents came out to greet them. Sam ran out of the car towards them, wagging his tail.

"Hello Sam." Tony's Dad made a fuss over him.

Tony's parents gave him a big hug.

"Mum, Dad, this is Amy."

"It is lovely to finally meet you, dear; we have heard so much about you. Come in and make yourself comfortable," Tony's mum said as she beckoned them inside.

"These are for you." Amy handed over the gifts to Tony's Mum.

"That is so kind of you Amy, thank you. Lunch will be ready soon. Tony, show Amy the garden and let Sam have a run around."

"Mum is very proud of her garden," Tony told Amy.

"I can understand why," replied Amy as they walked outside. "There are so many different colourful flowers, they smell gorgeous. I love the oriental water feature and the little bridge that goes over it. It feels so calming and peaceful."

"Mum and Dad spend a lot of time out here."

"You can tell. It looks very much loved."

"Just as you are Amy," Tony said, as he gave her a long romantic kiss.

A moment later, Tony's mum called out, "Tony, Amy, lunch is ready." Amy and Tony slowly made their way back into the house.

"You have a delightful garden," Amy told Tony's mum.

"Thank you, Amy. We like to spend time looking after it. We are both retired now, so we have plenty of time on our hands. Tony, your sister and brothers send their apologies for not being here; they will call you soon."

"They are always so busy."

"And so are you. It would be good to see more of all of you. Do you have any brothers and sisters, Amy?"

Amy could feel that knot in her stomach.

"Yes, I have a brother, Josh, but he died years ago."

"I am sorry to hear that Amy. So, is it just you and your parents?"

Amy looked at Tony for help.

"Mum, Amy's parents also died when she was young."

There was an awkward silence.

"Dad, how is it going down at the allotment?"

"Very well son. I have a new batch of potatoes and runner beans coming through."

"Dad grows his own vegetables," Tony told Amy.

"Are these yours that we are eating?" Amy asked.

"Yes, they are. What do you think of them?"

"They taste delicious. You cannot beat homegrown vegetables."

"I will take you to the allotment when you next visit. You can see what I am growing."

"I would like that very much." Amy smiled.

After lunch, Amy offered to help with the washing up.

"I will not hear of it. Amy, you are our guest. Go and sit down in the conservatory with Tony and I will bring out a pot of tea."

Meanwhile, Tony's Dad brought out the photo album.

"Not the photo album!" Tony cringed.

Tony's dad sat down next to Amy.

"Tony was a real little rascal when he was a young boy, always getting up to mischief. I remember when he was five years old, he tried climbing up the small tree that we had in the garden. It was way out of his reach, but Tony was not going to give up, so he went into the house and pulled a chair from under the table, took it out into the garden, climbed it and reached up as far as he could before falling and scraping his knees."

"Thank you for that dad!"

Amy could not stop laughing. By this time, she was feeling relaxed and at ease. The afternoon went extremely well. After a few more hours, it was time to leave.

"Do you have to go so soon? It feels like you have only just got here."

"I know Mum, the day has passed by fast. That is because we had such good company."

"Well, do not leave it so long next time. It has been a pleasure meeting you Amy. Will you come again?"

"I would like that very much. Thank you for a wonderful lunch."

Tony hugged his parent's goodbye whilst Amy and Sam waited in the car.

On the drive home, Tony looked over at Amy.

"Are you okay? You look so lost. Did you not enjoy today?"

"I had a wonderful day. Your parents are lovely. I am just missing my mum."

"I am sorry if Mum made you feel uncomfortable asking about your family. I should have told her beforehand."

"Yes, I did feel anxious, but I have to start talking about them at some point. I cannot keep avoiding it."

"Do you want to stay over at mine tonight? We can get a takeaway dinner and watch a film," Tony suggested.

"I would like that. Thank you for today Tony. It has been perfect."

Chapter 15

Amy had an amazing weekend with Tony after visiting his parents, and was back at work. In the evening there was another session planned with Mary Beth. Amy worked hard all day at work and went straight to her session afterwards.

"Hi Amy. Come in and make yourself comfortable. Can I get you something to drink?" Mary Beth asked.

"I am OK, thank you."

Amy felt a little embarrassed after the last time.

"How was your weekend?"

"It was very relaxing. I met Tony's parents for the first time."

"How did that go?"

"Really well. There was an anxious moment when his mum asked about my family. Tony saved the day as always."

"And how have the nightmares been?"

"I am still getting them, and the image is always the same. Tony recognises the signs, and he manages to wake me out of them before it properly starts. I do feel guilty though."

"Never feel guilty Amy. You have lived with trauma for years. I am sure Tony understands."

"He is such a big support for me, but, when I sleep alone, I wake up in a panic."

"That is because you know when he is there, he will wake you up, so subconsciously you feel safe. Let us do the session and talk again afterwards."

Mary Beth went through the same routine. Amy was slightly uncomfortable with the healing, but she surprisingly remained calm and composed.

"Well, that was a massive improvement. How did you find it?"

"I love meditation. I can zone out and feel at ease. Until my mind starts to wander, and I see the images, but today has been the best so far."

"I must say Amy. When I was going over your chakras the energy was really flowing lovely. There is still a slight blockage, but the results we are getting have been phenomenal," Mary Beth said proudly. "I know how much you enjoy meditation. Have you managed to do any at home?"

"Not as much as I would have liked."

"What I want to suggest is going on a meditation retreat. There is one that is specifically for people that have gone through emotional trauma. It is an amazing centre in the countryside where it is peaceful and quiet. I think you will benefit from it. And Tony."

"I like the sound of that. When is the next available date?"

"It is available next weekend. Talk it over with Tony, let me know and I will book it for you."

"That will be good."

"Well done Amy. You have come a very long way."

"Thank you, Mary Beth. I will call you tomorrow."

Amy left feeling uplifted and rather relaxed.

***

As Amy arrived home she was in a cheerful mood, better than she had felt in a long time.

"You seem happy," Tara commented as Amy walked through the door. "Did you have a good session with Mary Beth?"

"Yes, I did. For the first time, I did not feel anxious about what was going to happen, and I kept calm all the way through," Amy said proudly.

"Amy, that is fantastic news. No wonder why you are feeling happy."

"Mary Beth suggested that Tony and I go on a meditation retreat next weekend."

"How do you feel about that?"

"I want to go. I love meditation. I think Tony will enjoy it too."

"Rather you than me!" Tara laughed.

"It would do you the world of good Tara. Calm you down."

"I do not need to calm down thank you very much. I love being me!" Tara had the biggest cheeky grin on her face.

"What time are you leaving on Saturday?"

"It will be an early start. I must be on the ship by nine thirty, ready to set sail by four o clock in the afternoon. There is a lot to do before I go. Do not forget our girly day on Friday."

"Do not worry Tara, I have not forgotten," Amy promised.

"I will let you get on. I am going to sort out my room."

"Are you feeling OK Tara?" Amy teased.

"You are such a comic Amy," Tara said sarcastically.

Amy phoned Tony to tell him how the session went, and what Mary Beth suggested about the retreat.

"I think that it's a good idea Amy. Go ahead and book it. Having a weekend away in the country sounds blissful."

"Tara leaves on Saturday, so I am taking Friday off work to spend the day with her. Do you want to come over when she goes and do some meditation?"

"Is that what they call it these days!"

"Slow down tiger. Meditation first." Amy giggled.

"I will be there." Tony made a roaring noise making Amy laugh, said goodbye and hung up.

Amy made a cup of tea and went to bed singing along the way.

***

The next day Amy decided she wanted to start focusing on meditation and getting her mindset in the right place. To understand more, Amy needed to speak with Mary Beth. She gave her a phone call that evening after work.

"Amy, how can I help?"

"Mary Beth, can you book the retreat for me and Tony please? It sounds just what I need right now. I want to focus on meditation and concentrate on my mindset. Can you explain more about the techniques I should use?"

"Amy, this is good to know. So, to get you in the right mindset, start by pushing out any negative thoughts about the past that cannot be changed. It is OK to express your feelings and emotions. Do not deny what happened. But, choosing to move forward and be in control of your mind is an important part of your wellbeing. Focus on the positive. Surround your words and images with love and gratitude. Then proceed with meditation. Do just the same as we do in our sessions. How does that sound?"

"Thank you, Mary Beth. Tony is coming over on the weekend, and we will spend some time doing this."

"Let me know if you need any help. Come and see me when you get back from the retreat."

After her telephone conversation with Mary Beth, Amy was feeling positive and looking forward to the retreat with Tony. Tara was out for the evening, and Amy decided to take the opportunity to play the meditation CD. Making herself comfortable, Amy closed her eyes and took three deep breaths and slowly released them. Asking for guidance and protection, Amy continued listening to the meditation. Feeling peaceful and relaxed, it did not take long for Amy's mind to start wandering. Images came through that she was trying to avoid. Getting agitated, Amy opened her eyes. Wiping the beads of sweat from her brow, she got a glass of water.

"Please, just go away!" Amy shouted.

At that point, Tara walked through the door.

"That's charming!"

"Sorry Tara, I did not mean for you to go away. I was meditating and saw the images again."

"You mean you want the images to go away."

"Yes. I do not even need to be asleep now. I thought if I did meditation at home, it would help as it really relaxes me."

"Maybe that is it. You are too relaxed, as if you were sleeping. Speak to Mary Beth."

"I did earlier. She went through the routine with me."

"And did you follow her instructions?"

"I think so. How hard can it be?"

"Amy, you have to get your head in the right mindset before you start. Did you do that?"

Amy thought about it for a while.

"Now that you mention it, no, I did not. I just went straight into it."

"There you go. That is where it went wrong."

Amy looked at Tara suspiciously.

"How come suddenly you are an expert? You know nothing about mindset and meditation. You do not even like it."

"Amy, because it is not right for me, it does not mean that I have not taken any notice. I see how much more relaxed you are when you come back from your sessions with Mary Beth. Well, most of the time, unless you have had a meltdown."

"Tara. Thanks."

"You are welcome." Tara laughed.

"Seriously. I have been doing my research, to understand and help you. Only if I have to."

"Tara. Stop it."

"Amy. I am joking."

"I wish you would not Tara. It is not a good feeling."

"Amy, you know what I am like."

"There is a time and place for your jokes, Tara, and today is not one of them."

"Sorry Amy. I have been reading about mindset and meditation. And I always want to help you."

"I know you do Tara. You have been my rock all these years. I am truly grateful."

"Soul sisters, is that what they call it?"

Amy could not help but giggle.

"Yes. Soul sisters."

"Would you like a cup of tea?"

"That sounds great."

Tara went and put the kettle on. Amy sat wondering when this would end.

***

Tara was due back on the ship the following day. Amy had planned a girly day out for the two of them.

"Tara, are you ready? The taxi is here!" Amy shouted.

Tara ran down the stairs like an excited child.

"Where are we going?"

"I thought we would go into town and start off with breakfast at that lovely cafe you like and then some serious retail therapy, followed by lunch at The Lounge, more shopping, and then back home to watch a film of your choice. How does that sound?"

"Sounds like I need to go away more often!" grinned Tara.

Amy and Tara's first stop were to have breakfast at Josie's Cafe. Tara had fried eggs, bacon, sausage, beans, and toast. Amy chose a healthier option of porridge with cinnamon and honey.

"That was lovely," Tara said, placing her hands over her stomach satisfied.

"Now, let us hit those shops."

Amy and Tara had so much fun trying on different clothes and makeup. They laughed all day long, acting like two school kids. Returning home exhausted, they flopped onto the sofa.

"Amy that was the best day, thank you."

"I am going to miss you so much Tara."

"And I will miss you too. But you have Tony to keep you company now. He will look after you."

"I know, but it is not the same without you here."

"You mean nobody to shout at. 'Keep the house tidy Tara!'" Tara joked.

Amy roared with laughter.

"Am I that annoying?" she asked.

"Just a bit. You keep me on my toes, and I love you for it. I am way too tired to watch the film. Do you mind if I go to bed? I have an early start."

"Of course not. Have a good sleep."

Tara hugged Amy and went to bed.

Amy sat reflecting on when she first met Tara. As a frightened young girl living in foster care and starting a new school after her parents and Josh had died... Tara took Amy under her wing, and they had been best friends ever since. Amy could never imagine life without Tara. It was still early. Amy put on her pyjamas, made a cup of tea and settled down to watch the film before bed.

***

Early the next morning, Tara woke up excited about getting back on the cruise. She was going to miss being at home with Amy but singing on the ships was her passion. There was a gentle knock on her bedroom door. Amy slowly opened it.

"Tara, can I come in?"

"Amy, you are almost in any way!" chuckled Tara.

"Do you need any help packing?"

"I am nearly done thank you. Just these last bits to put in."

Amy sat on Tara's bed and looked at the mess. Tara could see her face.

"Amy, do not say a word."

Amy put her hand over her mouth.

Tara playfully jumped on Amy, tickling her. They lay on the bed looking at the ceiling, breathing hard with laughter.

"I am going to miss this Tara."

"I will be coming back. You do know that." Tara smiled. "I could hear you crying again last night. Another nightmare?"

Amy sat up.

"Yes. Some nights are more vivid than others. Meditation and relaxation music has helped, so has the energy healing. I pray that one day the nightmares will end."

"Amy they will. Keep to the mindset every day. You must focus on positive things. Remember the good times and memories. Saying this mantra may help: I open my heart and shine only love, forgiving those from up above. My eyes see the good, and in my mind, I release. What no longer serves me, brings me inner peace."

There was silence as Tara got up from the bed, wiped a tear from her eye and continued packing her last bits.

Amy looked at Tara and her mouth opened wide in disbelief. This was so out of character for Tara as she always joked about everything.

"Tara, where did that come from?"

"A book that I have been reading. I told you I had been doing my research."

"That was more than coming from a book. You said that with such passion and from the heart."

"Amy, I do have a heart, you know. But do not tell anyone." Tara laughed, making light of it.

"I love you so much." Amy threw her arms around Tara, giving her the biggest hug.

"Amy, I love you too. But I cannot breathe!"

Amy let go of her and smiled.

"My taxi will be here in five minutes. I need to go."

Tara zipped up her suitcase and dragged it down the stairs.

"Do you have everything?"

"I think so." The taxi arrived.

"Let me know how the meditation retreat goes. Speak to you soon. Love you."

Amy waved to Tara and closed the door. Thinking about what Tara had said earlier, Amy knew she had to beat this. Not just for herself, but for the people that had supported her, especially Tara and Tony.

***

Later that evening, Tony came over and brought a Chinese takeaway with him and some flowers for Amy. She had already informed him of her events with Tara that morning. Amy put the flowers into a vase, got some plates out of the cupboard and served up the food.

"This Chinese food is delicious. Thank you for bringing it and I love my flowers. Is Sam OK at home by himself?"

"I decided to drop him off at a friend's house. We do dog sitting for each other when needed."

"You do know you can always bring Sam here when you stay over. I love seeing him."

"Thank you, I will do that in the future. How are you feeling about the retreat next weekend?"

"I am looking forward to the peaceful and relaxing surroundings and being in the right mindset. Something that I am going to work hard on. How about you?"

"It will be like a breath of fresh air for both of us."

"Will you still do this meditation with me later?"

"Of course." Tony replied.

Amy and Tony finished their meal and enjoyed the evening playing board games. Before they settled down for the night, they got into their pyjamas and made themselves comfortable. They laid in bed whilst Amy put on the CD, began doing some mindset exercises and went into meditation. Listening to the sound of the guides calming voice and gentle music they peacefully relaxed and enjoyed just being in the moment together. When the CD had finished, Tony opened his eyes and looked over at Amy. She was fast asleep. Tony turned the bedside lamp off and went to sleep too.

***

The next morning the light was shining through the curtains. Amy woke up feeling peaceful. Tony was still sleeping. Amy got out of bed, went downstairs, and sat in the lounge. On the sideboard was a photograph of Amy's mum and Josh. On the other side was a picture of her foster parents. Amy touched both and thought about the good memories she had shared with them all. Amy picked up the pictures, held them close to her heart, and gently whispered, "I can do this."

Tony woke up and went downstairs to find Amy holding the pictures. There was no need for words. Placing his arm around Amy, she laid her head on his shoulder and closed her eyes.

Chapter 16

Every evening before bedtime, Amy would go through her routine of mindset and meditation to relax her mind and body before going to sleep. Even when there was a quiet moment at work, Amy would take five minutes to focus. She was determined to beat the horrific nightmares and be free.

The weekend was here, and Amy and Tony were on their way to the meditation retreat.

"How are you feeling about this weekend Amy?" Tony asked.

"Not as anxious as I thought I would be. I am just looking forward to relaxing and spending time with you in the peaceful surroundings of the countryside."

"How about you? What are your thoughts about it?"

"I think it will be beneficial for us both, clearing our minds from the madness of the week. My main expectations are that you will find some release from your nightmares."

"I hope so too."

An hour later, they arrived at their destination. The long gravel road leading up to the manor house took a few minutes. All that was around were fields of lush green grass and the most delightful looking flowers and trees. Tony parked and took the bags out of the car. They booked in at the reception and were given the keys to their room. It was beautifully decorated and the view from the window was captivating. The agenda for the weekend was placed on the desk, starting with a welcome gathering before the evening meal.

After they had unpacked their bags, Amy and Tony went for a walk around the grounds. It was so quiet and peaceful. They met other guests on their walks and politely said hello.

"Tony look, they have a lake with swans."

On the lake were little waterfalls that cascaded over the rocks... The sun glistened over the water, sparkling like tiny diamonds. It was just perfect.

On their walk, they came across a nook set back in amongst the trees, along with a carved bench. Amy and Tony sat on the bench and absorbed the sun and tranquillity.

"Amy, can you hear that?"

"What am I listening to?"

"Nothing. It is so peaceful. I am happy to just sit here for the rest of the day."

"Me too. Tony look, there is a plaque," Amy said, getting closer to take a better look at it.

"What does it say?"

"Release what hurts your heart beautiful soul. There is only you and me here. I will listen and never judge."

"That is a powerful statement. Who wrote it?"

"There is no name. Sounds like it was meant for me to see," Amy commented.

"We had better head back and get ready for the welcome gathering."

Tony took Amy by the hand and they slowly made their way back to the manor house.

After having a short nap, Amy and Tony got ready to go down for dinner and the welcome talk.

There was a very large and spacious room on the first floor called Serenity, where the gathering was to be held. The smell of lavender along the corridor was inviting. Amy and Tony entered the room. There were around twenty other people at the retreat. The last person to arrive was the organiser of the event.

"Welcome everyone. My name is Helen. I will be your instructor for the weekend. I will not keep you for long, you must be hungry after your journey and ready for dinner. The intention and purpose of the weekend is so that you can be away from noise and distraction, to focus, knowing that this is a safe place to be yourself, and search deep within, releasing anything that is stopping you from moving forward in life. We will concentrate on our mindset and how to change habits and thoughts whilst paying attention to our feelings and emotions. There will be multiple meditation sessions over the weekend. We even have a yoga class if you wish to attend. We are all here for different reasons, and your experience is a personal journey. Do take advantage of the amazing grounds around the manor. The first session starts at ten thirty in the morning after breakfast. If you have any questions, I will be in the office until nine o'clock this evening. Enjoy your dinner and I look forward to our session in the morning."

Everyone quietly left the room and headed to the restaurant for dinner. Amy and Tony found a table to sit at. Gentle music played in the background. They took a few minutes to take in the atmosphere of the dining room and choose their meal from the menu.

"The welcome was informative. How do you feel about the sessions tomorrow?" Tony asked as he poured himself and Amy a glass of water from the jug on the table.

"I am looking forward to it in a nervous way. It is the not knowing."

"The best thing to do is take each session as it comes. It can only be positive. Let us enjoy our meal and have an early night."

"I'm not feeling very tired."

"Who said anything about sleeping?" Tony gave Amy a cheeky smile.

"Tony, stop it!" Amy could feel her cheeks blushing.

Amy gave a quick glance around the restaurant, making sure nobody had heard. Just then, the waiter arrived with their meal. Tony raised a glass of water to Amy.

"Here is to change and transformation," he said.

Amy smiled, praying that Tony was right.

***

The following morning, after breakfast, Amy and Tony headed to the serenity room for the first meditation session and were greeted by Helen.

"Good morning everyone. I am happy to see you all. Before we begin I want to mention that if at any time you feel overwhelmed and wish to leave the room, I ask that you be respectful to everyone else and exit quietly. Are there any questions before we start?" Helen paused briefly, then continued, "I would like you to seat yourself in a comfortable position either sitting on the cushions or on a chair. Close your eyes, bring awareness to the breath, take a deep breath in, and slowly release it." Everyone was doing as instructed. "And repeat this two more times. Know that you are safe and surrounded in a bubble of love. Imagine you are on a beach. The golden sand feels soft underneath your feet. The sun makes your body warm and relaxed. You are happy and smiling. Pay attention to the sound of the sea as it gently goes out and flows back in. Now focus on your intentions. What do you want to let go and be free of? Take your time, there is no rush."

Amy was feeling so relaxed and calm until it was time to let go. Her nightmares came to light and the same image reappeared. Starting to feel overwhelmed, Amy quietly left the room and took herself outside to get some fresh air. Heading towards the nook they had discovered earlier, Amy sat on the carved bench and read the plaque again. *Release what hurts your heart beautiful soul. There is only you and me here. I will listen and never judge.*

Amy sat there and cried. *Why can I not let go of these images and the pain in my heart?* she thought. Amy felt a hand gently touch her shoulder. It was Tony.

"I thought you would be here. Are you OK?"

"Not really. Why is this so difficult to do?"

"I wish I could give you the answers Amy. Talk to Helen. She will be able to tell you."

Amy and Tony headed back to the manor house.

When they got there, the session had finished.

"Amy are you OK?" Helen asked.

Amy explained to Helen what she has been going through with the nightmares and images.

"Amy, have you ever pursued help for your emotional trauma before?"

"No, I am seeing a spiritual healer, Mary Beth. She has been helping me and recommended that I come here."

"I know Mary Beth. She is an amazing lady and is excellent at what she does, helping so many people on their healing journey. Have you been to see a councillor or therapist about your nightmares?"

"No, I had never seen anyone until I met Tony. We have been looking for someone but did not find anyone that I felt was right for me. Then I met Mary Beth."

"How do you find talking about what happened in the past to cause these nightmares?"

"I did not find it easy at all. But since seeing Mary Beth, it has definitely helped."

"I am glad to hear that. In this afternoon's session we will be talking about mindfulness and mindset, looking at how it can help through difficult times. Go and have some lunch. We will meet for the next session at 3pm."

Amy and Tony went for lunch. Amy sat playing with the food on her plate. Tony could see she was preoccupied.

"Amy, talk to me. What are you thinking?"

"I cannot see this ever ending. Maybe I am just a lost cause."

"That is not true. You have come a long way, do not start giving up. Amy, you have to believe that you can beat this."

"Tony I am trying. Something keeps holding me back."

"Amy, you are holding yourself back. You must trust and have faith that it is going to happen. I do understand that it is difficult for you. I really do. We are all here to help you."

Amy smiled at Tony, not feeling very convinced.

After lunch, they went for a walk around the grounds before going to the next session.

"Welcome back everyone. In this session we will briefly look at the three M's: mindfulness, mindset, and meditation. Some of you might have already practiced these at home. Let us start with mindfulness. The act of being aware of your thoughts and emotions, about being present now without judgement, not thinking about the past and accepting your feelings, whatever they are. Then you have mindset. When you focus on positive beliefs, your use of words and actions will change. You will become a better version of yourself by feeling happier, more confident and a stronger person. And lastly, there is meditation. By using a set of techniques, this practice can increase mental peace and calm, encouraging healing and positive change. Each one of these practices is a fabulous tool for our wellbeing, but the one important thing they have in common is breath work. Breathing exercises are the main ingredient. When we breathe deeply, it lowers stress and sends a message to the brain to calm down and relax. Leaving us feeling in a better place. I hope that all makes sense. Are there any questions?" She paused. "So, to finish off this session, we are going to do some breathing exercises. Make yourself comfortable. When you are ready, place one hand on your chest connecting you to your heart centre and the other on your belly. Close your eyes and take a deep breath in through the nose and slowly release it out of the mouth so that you can feel the air pushing the hand on your abdomen. Repeat it again, and one last time. Gently open your eyes and have a big stretch and smile. You are all looking very relaxed and should have a peaceful sleep tonight. Tomorrow is our last session. We will be incorporating all three practices and doing some release work. Thank you for coming to the session. Enjoy the rest of your evening and I will see you at eleven in the morning. I will be around for a while if you want to ask me any questions."

There was a lot of chatter and smiling faces as everyone left.

"That breath work was amazing. How did you find it?" Tony asked Amy.

"I felt better coming out of there than when I went in. I need to get into the habit of doing these breathing exercises. The session was good. I enjoyed learning more about the three M's."

"Let us go mad and order a bottle of elder flower wine with our meal this evening." Tony laughed.

"That sounds wonderful, but I need to take a shower first."

"Me too… We can always save water and share." Tony winked at

Amy.

"Tony, you have been a bit frisky since we got here!" Amy mocked.

"It must be the calming atmosphere around here."

"Well, if that's what it does to you, I better keep my distance!" Amy teased, as she pushed Tony and ran off.

"Come here you!" Tony laughed as he ran after Amy, both of them giggling like two naughty children.

***

Amy and Tony did not leave their room all evening.

"Tony it is seven am. Did we really sleep all that time?"

"Well, not all the time," Tony grinned.

Amy threw a pillow at him.

"We even missed dinner! No wonder I am so hungry. Let us go have breakfast."

Amy leapt out of bed, took a quick shower, and got dressed, and waited for Tony to get ready too.

After eating a big meal, Amy and Tony went for a leisurely walk around the garden.

"It is so calming here. Can you smell the scent coming from the flowers? It is pure bliss." Amy inhaled the aroma.

"I know what you mean. I must say that being here has certainly done me a world of good. How have you found it?"

"I have not felt this relaxed in a very long time, but I was hoping for too much."

"What do you mean?" Tony asked, as they went and sat by the

lake.

"My expectations were too high. I was expecting a miracle to happen and that my nightmares would just disappear."

"Amy, it is going to take time. Look at how far you have come. Taking the biggest step was getting help and that is a real achievement. Do not be so hard on yourself. There is one session left, just see how it goes. Speaking of going, I need to go to the bathroom. I will meet you back at the house."

Amy walked a bit further and was drawn to the nook again. She sat on the carved bench, closed her eyes, and started to do breathing exercises, using the mindset techniques, whilst repeating the words *I am free*. Amy heard a voice whisper, "Yes, you are."

Amy opened her eyes and looked around, but no one was there. She sat down for a few more minutes and walked back to the house.

Tony was waiting for Amy by the entrance.

"Are you ready?"

Amy nodded, and they joined the rest of the group. Helen welcomed everyone.

"For our final session, we are going to release and forgive."

Amy instantly felt the tension in her stomach and lowered her head. Forgiving her father was the one thing she vowed never to do.

"One of the biggest reasons why we find it hard to let go and release, is forgiveness. We tell ourselves, why should I forgive? And my reply to that is why not? Who does it serve by holding on to anger, hatred, resentment, and pain? Nothing can change past events, but we do have the choice to move forward. Forgiveness does not mean that what that person or situation did is right or that we will forget. It merely means that we choose to no longer hold on to it and be free from our prison within. Unlocking the door so that we can rebuild our lives."

Amy kept her head low as the tears streamed down her face. Tony held her hand to reassure her that it was OK.

"I ask you to make yourself comfortable as we prepare for meditation."

Whilst everyone was getting ready, Helen walked amongst the group playing her Tibetan singing bowl. The powerful healing sounds that came from it echoed around the room, helping to release any stress and anxiety before proceeding with the meditation.

Helen sat comfortably on the floor, put some quiet, relaxing music on and began meditation.

"When you are feeling comfortable, close your eyes, take a deep breath in through your nose, fill your lungs, and exhale the air gently through your mouth. Repeat this slowly two more times. Listening to the soothing sound of music makes you feel calm and relaxed. Pay attention to your breathing. Know that you are safe and surrounded by a bubble of love. Now, take your time and think about what has been troubling you, draining your energy. You are in a safe space. Allow those thoughts and feelings to come forward. Tell them what it has done to you. I am going to be silent for a few minutes, but I am still here."

After a while, Helen looked around the room and could see the pain, sadness, and anger on some people's faces.

"I want you to place your left hand on your chest and put your right hand on top of it. It is time to open your heart to forgiveness and set yourself free. Release and let it go."

Amy was getting agitated by the image appearing in her mind and finding it difficult. She sat there shaking her head. *I will not forgive you.*

Tony could hear Amy's sobs. He sat in front of her and held her hands and whispered, "Amy, it is time to let go."

Amy opened her eyes and looked at Tony. He smiled lovingly at her and bowed his head. She closed her eyes, and it was not long until an image came to her. It was her dad. He stepped forward. Mum and Josh were standing at his side. He held out his hand and said, "Please forgive me Amy."

She looked at Mum and Josh. They were smiling and nodded their heads in approval. Slowly reaching out her hand, and with an open heart, feeling calm, Amy spoke to her father.

"I forgive you Dad."

Mum, Dad, and Josh smiled and waved goodbye as they started to fade away. Amy let out a big sigh and opened her eyes.

"Tony, I did it! I forgave him."

"I know. I heard you." Tony wiped the tears off his face.

"Mum and Josh were so happy. I cannot believe that I did it."

By this time, the whole room had come alive. There were so many happy tear-stained faces. Helen had not seen this kind of reaction in one of her sessions from so many people before. It made her emotional, feeling the massive shift of energy in the room.

Gathering herself together and calming everyone down, Helen continued, "Okay, that was truly amazing. Seeing so many smiling faces makes my heart jump with joy. I know that it was so hard for some of you to feel that vulnerable. Today you have taken an incredible step on your journey. It will continue to be a work in progress, so be gentle with yourself. Always go back to using breathing techniques. Remember the three M's: mindset is paramount. Staying positive and focused is the key to a happy and fulfilled life. Mindfulness helps reduce anxiety and stress. Be in the present moment and not in the past. Meditation has many benefits, it can help you to feel calm and at peace through difficult times. Taking time to be silent and still is like a breath of fresh air. You will find your own way and techniques of doing these things. Just go with the flow and let your intuition be your guide. We will now end with a prayer of thanks. Close your eyes and place your hands together in prayer, holding them to your heart.

"Thank you, heavenly guides, for being present with us on this journey of release, healing, and celebration. Giving us strength by opening our hearts to forgiveness and freeing us from past events. Moving forward to a brighter, healthier, happier life. With gratitude, thank you.

"Sit in silence for a few minutes and when you are ready, open your eyes. I have really enjoyed our time together and thank you for allowing me into your personal space. If I can be of service in the future, you have my details. With love, peace, and blessings, I wish you a safe journey home."

Everyone left the room smiling and feeling happy. Amy and Tony went to their room and packed. Holding Amy in his arms, he looked deep into her eyes, feeling an even stronger love.

"I am so proud of you Amy. That took a lot of strength. How do you feel?"

"I feel like the luckiest girl in the world to have the most amazing, understanding, and loving man in my life. Thank you, Tony, for standing by me through all my crazy times and listening when I was at my lowest. Being here has given me my life back. I can finally move on."

"Shall we make a move? There will be two people happy to hear the good news."

Amy had the biggest smile on her face. She was so excited to tell Tara and Mary Beth. Tony packed the car.

"Tony, do you mind if I take a quick walk down to the nook before we leave?"

"Of course not, take your time. I will be waiting right here."

Amy went to the nook and sat on the carved bench. She took a few deep breaths and reflected on her time at the manor house.

Amy read the plaque one last time: *Release what hurts your heart beautiful soul. There is only you and me here. I will listen and never judge.*

Amy smiled and whispered thank you. Amy turned to walk away when a gentle breeze brushed her face. It felt warm and comforting but strange as there was no wind. Making her way down the pathway, Amy stopped and looked back. The nook had disappeared. It was as if she knew that it was a special place just for her.

Tony was waiting by the car.

"Are you ready?"

Amy took one last look around.

"Yes, let's go home."

***

When they got back, Tony unpacked the car and took Amy's bags inside.

"Thank you for the best weekend. I feel like a whole new person." Amy could not stop smiling.

"It changed us both. It certainly made me rethink my life."

"What do you mean?"

"To not knock myself out working all hours. To embrace every moment. To value what really matters and cherish those you love. It clarified a lot."

"I think we should celebrate. Take your things home, pick up Sam and I will order some food."

"That sounds good to me. I love you Amy. I really do."

"And I love you too. Now go, so I can unpack."

"I will be back in a couple of hours," Tony said, as he left the room.

Amy had to pinch herself. Is this nightmare really over?

***

Later that evening, Amy and Tony had a wonderful meal. Sam was not left out. He was happy with his dog treats. After they cleared the plates, Tony took Sam for a quick walk and Amy prepared some hot chocolate for when they got back.

"It is getting a bit chilly out there." Tony rubbed his hands together. Sam laid on the blanket and went to sleep.

"This will warm you up." Amy handed Tony a cup of hot chocolate.

"Just what I needed, thank you."

"Tony, are you OK? You seem a bit anxious. That is normally my job!" Amy chuckled.

"I am fine. But there is something I want to say. I just need to find the right words…"

"Tony, what is it? It is me, isn't it. You found the weekend too much. Oh, God, I am so sorry." Amy started to panic.

"Amy calm down! Everything is good."

"So, what is it then?"

"I am just going to come out and say it." Tony's hands were getting sweaty.

"I do not want to hear it." Amy turned away.

"Amy. Look at me."

Amy turned around. Tony was on one knee.

Amy put her hand to her mouth and gasped.

"From the day I saw you, all wet and angry, I knew I had fallen in love with you there and then, thanks to Sam."

Sam's ears twitched. He lifted his head and went back to sleep.

"I always thought that love at first sight was something only in fairy tales until I met you. Everything about you fills my heart with joy. This weekend has been a revelation. My love for you has grown even stronger and confirmed to me that I want to spend the rest of my life with you. Amy, will you marry me?"

Amy still had her hand over her mouth and stood in silence and shock, unable to reply.

"Amy, I am getting a cramp in my leg." Tony nervously laughed.

Suddenly, she let out an almighty squeal.

Sam woke up barking. Tony jumped up quickly.

"Yes! Of course I will. Are you sure?"

"Amy, you scared the life out of me, and Sam."

"I am sorry. I was not expecting that. Tony, I would love to be your wife. This weekend could not get any better! I am so happy."

Tony took a box from his pocket and opened it. He placed a ring on Amy's finger.

Amy began to cry.

"I hope they are happy tears?" Tony smiled.

"They are definitely happy tears. Tony, it is stunning. But how did you manage to get it in such a short time?

"I have a confession to make. I bought it a few months ago. But you were in an awful place, it did not feel right. Now is the perfect time," Tony beamed.

"Yes, it is. I cannot wait to tell Tara!" Amy said excitedly.

"Not tonight. I want to have this moment just for us. Give her a call tomorrow."

Amy and Tony held each other for the longest time, savouring the moment. Amy's new chapter in her life had just begun.

Chapter 17

Amy woke up full of energy. The first thing she did was thank the universe for her new life and for sending her the man of her dreams. She looked over at Tony, still sleeping, and kissed him gently on the cheek. Amy went and made a cup of tea. Sam came bounding over to her.

"Morning Sam, did you sleep well?" She asked, scratching him behind the ears.

Amy sat drinking her tea, admiring the ring on her finger. She still could not believe that she was engaged. Eager to tell Tara, she gave her a call.

"Amy. Do you know what time it is?"

"Yes. Seven thirty."

"Maybe where you are. It is two thirty a.m. here."

"Tara, I am surprised you are in bed. I thought you would be partying for hours."

"Amy, I do not party all the time, you know. I hope you have a good reason for waking me up."

"I have two very good reasons."

Tara's tone of voice changed.

"What is wrong? Has something happened?"

Amy thought it would be fun to tease Tara.

"Yes, something has happened. I just do not know how to tell you."

Tara was getting worried now.

"Amy, please tell me."

"Well, you know me and Tony went on the retreat? I just cannot find the words Tara."

"Amy stop. Tell me."

Amy could hear the concern in Tara's voice and suddenly felt awful, so she decided to come clean.

"Tara, I have been teasing you. Nothing has happened. Well, it has, but nothing to worry about."

"Amy, you call me at a stupid hour just to tease me?"

Tara's tone was not a very happy one.

"Sorry Tara. But I do have the best news."

Amy then explained to Tara everything that had happened at the retreat.

"Amy that is fantastic, I am so happy for you. It has been a long time. You can now finally move forward."

"Tara that is not all. Are you ready for this?"

"Yes, I am."

"Are you sitting down?"

"Amy, I am in bed, remember!"

"Oh yes. I forgot." Amy laughed. "Guess who is getting married?"

It was very quiet for a few minutes.

"Tara, are you still there?"

"Yes, I am just waiting for you to tell me who."

"Tara, it is me." Amy was disappointed.

"Got you!" Tara shrieked quietly, not to wake anyone. "Amy I am so excited. When did this happen?"

"Last night after we got back from the retreat. Tony was so nervous, bless him."

"When is the wedding? Am I, as your best friend in the world, a bridesmaid?"

"Of course you will be. I want to get married very soon. Tara, I have never been this happy."

"Amy, you deserve happiness more than anyone."

"I have you and Tony to thank for that, and Mary Beth."

"Amy, you did this. It was a matter of belief and strength. And you finally found it. I am so incredibly proud of you."

Amy wiped a tear trickling down her cheek.

"I better let you get back to sleep. Sorry I woke you up."

"How do you expect me to sleep now? I am so excited," Tara chuckled.

"I will let you know what the plans are when I discuss them with Tony. Love you Tara."

Amy put the phone down and sat there with the biggest smile on her face.

"Who were you talking to at this time of the morning? No, let me guess?" Tony yawned.

"I was so excited I woke Tara up. It was two thirty in the morning there."

"I can imagine her reaction," Tony grinned.

"Once she had calmed down and I told her about what

happened at the retreat and our engagement it was fine. Are you going to work today?"

"I will be after a cup of coffee and a big cuddle from my fiancée."

"I like the sound of that. Cuddle first, then coffee."

Amy felt so safe with Tony. Nothing would ever hurt her again.

"Tony, I know we only got engaged last night, but how would you feel about getting married as soon as we can? Unless you want to wait, of course."

"Why would I want to wait? I have never been so sure about anything. We can talk about it later. I have to take Sam back and get ready for work."

Amy waved to Tony and Sam as they left, closed the door, and danced around the room singing in jubilation whilst looking at her ring. Amy forgot about the time and was late getting ready for work. When she finally arrived, she was in a fantastic mood.

"Morning everyone, did you have a good weekend?" Amy beamed as she walked into the office.

"Yes, thank you," they replied.

"Your weekend must have been good with that big smile on your face," Gill commented.

"Actually, it was more than good." Amy held up her hand, showing off her new ring.

"Tony and I got engaged!"

Gill got up from her chair and looked closer at the ring.

"Amy it is gorgeous. So, when is the big day?"

"We are going to talk about it later but decided not to wait, so it will be soon. And you are all invited."

Mr Higgins came out of his office to see what all the fuss was about. Amy explained and showed him her ring.

"I am very happy for you Amy. Tony is a lucky man. Now, how about we get on with some work?"

Amy made Mr Higgins his usual cup of coffee and sat at her desk ready to start her day. The morning was busy with phone calls and paperwork. At one o clock, Amy took her lunch break. She bought a sandwich and a bottle of orange juice and sat on a bench to make a phone call to Mary Beth.

"Amy, how are you? How was the retreat?"

"That is what I wanted to talk to you about. May I come and see you after work?"

"Yes, of course. I look forward to seeing you."

Amy was excited about telling Mary Beth everything that had happened.

The afternoon flew by. Amy left the office and went to see Mary Beth. When Amy arrived, she stood at the door, remembering how nervous she felt on her first visit and how things had changed since that day.

"Amy, come in. It is so good to see you. How have you been?"

"Mary Beth, I have never felt better."

"Well, this sounds positive. Do tell me."

"As you know, Tony and I went on the retreat. It was an amazing place, so peaceful and calm. Helen was lovely. She spoke highly of you. The first day was intense. I expected some big changes to happen straight away, and it never did. We went through the three M's."

"And what were the three M's?" Mary Beth asked.

"Mindfulness, mindset, and meditation. I learned a lot from them. It was during the last session that things began to change. Helen talked about forgiveness. I became anxious and felt angry. The one thing I vowed never to do was forgive my father, but during the meditation I had an image of my dad standing in front of me asking to be forgiven. Mum and Josh were there too, smiling. Then he reached out his hand."

Amy could feel the emotions.

"Amy, it is OK."

"I held my hand out to his and forgave him."

Mary Beth wiped a tear from her cheek.

"And have the nightmares stopped?"

"Yes, they have. I can now go to sleep feeling at peace and free."

"I knew you could do it Amy."

"That is not all."

Mary Beth looked at Amy intrigued.

"Tony asked me to marry him." Amy showed Mary Beth the ring.

"Oh, my word. Amy, this is the best news. I am so proud and happy for you."

"I want to thank you Mary Beth, for not giving up on me."

"Amy, you did this. It was just a matter of believing in yourself, and a little divine intervention." Mary Beth winked at her.

"We would love for you to come to the wedding when we have set a date. It will be as soon as there is a church free."

"I would be very honoured Amy. Thank you. How about we

have one final session?"

Amy laid on the couch and closed her eyes. Mary Beth led the meditation giving thanks for the new beginnings, freedom, and inner peace in Amy's life and for releasing her from the prison within that had kept her trapped for many years. Mary Beth placed her hands above Amy's body, scanning her chakras. Amy had a smile on her face and a tiny tear trickled from the corner of her eye. Everything was peaceful and calm. All of Amy's chakras were in alignment and flowing freely.

"Amy, when you are ready, open your eyes."

Amy opened her eyes feeling so at peace. Slowing getting up from the couch, Mary Beth gave her a glass of water.

"You are glowing Amy; all tension and stress has completely left your face. You are shining."

"Thank you again Mary Beth. I will never forget you."

"It was a pleasure Amy. Keep practicing the three M's. I look forward to seeing you at your wedding."

Amy gave Mary Beth a big hug and left feeling the best she had ever felt.

***

"Amy, how on earth have you managed to organise a wedding in a few months?" Tara asked.

"It just fell into place. Every avenue I went down happened to be free. Tara, you are probably wondering where your bridesmaid dress is?"

"Well, yes. The wedding is in a few hours?"

"Before I reveal what I bought, I wanted to ask you something and I hope you are OK with it. Not only are you my best friend, sister, and pain in the backside. You have been through everything with me."

"Amy, what is it you are trying to say?"

"Do not be mad at me. Close your eyes."

Amy took Tara's outfit out of the wardrobe.

"OK, you can open them now."

Tara looked at her outfit.

"Amy is this what you want me to wear?"

"You hate it?"

"No, I am just a bit confused. That is not a bridesmaid dress."

"It will look amazing on you. And it fits the part."

"Amy, I have no idea what you are going on about."

"To walk me down the aisle!"

Tara did not know what to say.

"This is the most important day of my life and I do not have a dad to walk me down the aisle. You are my only family member. Will you do it?"

Tears started running down Tara's face.

"Now look what you have gone and done. I am going to have a red nose and a blotchy face."

"Is that a yes?" Amy smiled, handing Tara the outfit.

"What do you think?"

"Go and try it on. You are going to look stunning."

Whilst Tara was putting her outfit on, Amy spent a few moments quietly to herself. Looking out of her bedroom window, she took a deep breath and closed her eyes. Mum, Dad, and Josh were standing there in a vision blowing her kisses. Amy smiled knowing they were with her. She got into her wedding dress and placed the veil on her head. Tara came back into the room.

"What do you think?"

Amy turned around. Tara stood with her mouth slightly open.

"Amy, you look gorgeous. You are going to start me off again. Your parents and Josh will be so proud of you."

"Thank you, Tara."

"When Mrs R became sick, she gave me this box and asked me to give it to you on the day you got married. Her exact words were, 'Lose this, and I will come back from my grave and haunt you.' I thought that was a bit harsh, but you know what she was like."

Amy did not know whether to laugh or cry. Tara handed her the box... Amy opened it and inside was a necklace with an inscription on it: *Faith will be your strength.*

Amy took the necklace out of the box and put it on along with the one that her birth mum had given her on her thirteenth birthday and the bracelet from Josh. Amy held it to her lips and kissed it. Taking a deep breath, Amy nodded to Tara, indicating that she was ready to go.

"Amy, I need the toilet. You go ahead."

When Amy left the room, Tara closed the door.

"Ok God. You know I do not do this kind of thing so here goes. Thank you for helping Amy and giving her peace. For bringing Tony into her life. And for sending me the best friend anyone can ever have."

Tara bowed her head, and said amen, not knowing if that was

the correct thing to do. Feeling awkward, Tara gave a slight cough and went to leave the room. Catching a quick glance at herself in the mirror, she stood back.

"Tara, you look quite sexy in your suit." Smiling and giving herself a wink, she left to join Amy.

"I thought you fell down the toilet. What took you so long?" Amy laughed.

"Amy, never ask a lady such personal questions."

"Tara, find me a lady and I won't!"

They looked at each other and burst into laughter.

"Are you ready?" Tara held Amy's hand.

"I am ready."

They got into the car and headed to the church.

Waiting at the church for Amy to arrive, Tony was feeling nervous standing at the top of the aisle with his best man, James. It was a small wedding. Tony's family and a few friends attended. The music started to play. The vicar asked everyone to stand. Amy held Tara's arm as she walked down the aisle. Standing in the pews, Amy saw Mary Beth and some of her work colleagues and smiled at them. Tony turned around and, with tears in his eyes, gave Amy the biggest smile. Tara pulled the veil back from Amy's face, kissed her on the cheek and took her place with the others. Amy looked at Tony and whispered, "I love you." Everyone in the church wiped a tear from their eyes as Amy and Tony made their vows.

"Amy and Tony, I am happy to pronounce that you are now husband and wife. You may kiss your bride."

Tony kissed Amy to the sounds of clapping and cheering from the congregation. When walking back down the aisle, Amy looked up at where the organ player was sitting. Next to him, she saw three smiling silhouettes and on the other side of him, there were two others. Amy knew they were her mum, dad, Josh, and her foster parents. She smiled back at them. Her heart was bursting with happiness.

Outside in the glorious church gardens, everyone was chatting with each other whilst waiting for the photographer to set up his camera. Amy and Tara took a little stroll together.

"Well, this is it, the end of an era. We have certainly been through a lot together." Tara put her arm through Amy's.

"Tara it is not the end. It is just the beginning. Growing up with you by my side, always looking out for me, has been the best and I cannot thank you enough for helping me through the most awful times of my life. I will always need you, especially now."

Amy rubbed her hand across her belly.

Tara looked at Amy.

"Amy, are you pregnant?"

Amy smiled and nodded her head. Tara screeched with excitement.

"I am going to be an Aunty!"

"Tara, keep it to yourself for now. I have not told Tony yet."

"How long have you known?"

"I took the test this morning. It was positive."

"Amy, Tony is going to be thrilled. When will you tell him?"

"I will tell him later when we are on our own. Today has been the best day of my life, Tara."

"I love you Amy."

"And I love you too, Tara."

They hugged each other feeling so happy, not wanting to let go.

"Amy, Tara, it is time for the photos," Tony called out.

Amy and Tara gently wiped their cheeks from the tears and joined the others.

The photographer was ready. Just then, the church bells began to ring.

"OK, everyone say ding dong."

Laughing joyfully and saying 'ding dong', the photographer captured some of the most magical moments for Amy and Tony to remember.

This story may be fiction, but it could also well be true! Forgiveness and letting go of past events are not always easy. It takes time to heal the wounds. Working on your mindset plays an important role in finding that inner strength and peace so you can be free. Your wellbeing is what matters. Know you can do it... Just like Amy did.

Are you a prisoner within?

Did you know that writing is also another way of releasing our thoughts and feelings.

The written word is powerful, empowering and can help with emotional healing, giving you the freedom to take back control of your life.

Find out more about Jenny's write to release course at:
https://jennyscourse.thinkific.com/

You can purchase the write to release journal at:
https://www.jennyfordauthor.com/product-page/write-to-release-journal-pen

More by Jenny Ford:

Gabriella's Travels

The Rossini family live in a beautiful picturesque town called Positano, situated in the Campania region of Italy on the Amalfi coast where they own a small patisserie. There was mama Rosa and papa Joe and their four children, Anthony and Mario who were both married and Michael and their youngest and only daughter Gabriella. The Rossini patisserie was well known for its delicious pastries that had been passed down through generations of Rossini's using only the finest ingredients. The taste and textures of the pastries were divine. People would come from nearby towns to purchase them.

All four children helped in the patisserie, Anthony who was the eldest and Mario the second eldest helped papa make the pastries and Michael and Gabriella helped mama out front. Michael was heading off to Paris soon to finish his last year training to be a chef, his dream was to one day own his own restaurant and be one of the greatest chefs in Italy. He loved working at the patisserie and helped his parents out every time he came home. He had learnt a lot from his father but it's not where he wanted his career to be.

Gabriella was eighteen and just left school, she was quite a determined girl and knew what she wanted. Ever since she was a little girl she would say to her family, "When I'm old enough I want to travel all around Europe and explore all the different cultures." Her family would laugh.

"No Bella," papa would say. "You will work here in the family business; this will all be yours one day."

I'll be an old lady by the time that happens she thought to herself.

186

I will go to Europe; I will save every euro I get. And that is exactly what she did.

Gabriella's parents started to pay her for working in the patisserie when she was twelve years old. It was only a few euros but as she got older the money went up, and was paid even more in the high season when it got really busy. She also did extra work in the evenings helping students with their English language as Gabriella's English was excellent.

In her spare time Gabriella would study the map of Europe and mark off all the places she wanted to visit.

"Gabby you're not really going to do it?" her friends would say.

"Of course I am I want to travel before I get married so I can then tell my children about all the wonderful exciting places I have seen."

"Your parents will go mad!" added Maria. Maria was Gabriella's best friend; they had known each other ever since kindergarten.

"I know," replied Gabriella, "but by the time I'm twenty I would have saved enough money and then I'm off."

Gabriella worked hard at the patisserie working all the hours that she could. She would fit in as many English classes just so she could earn extra money for her travels.

It was the weekend, and Maria came to see Gabriella.

"Hey let's go to the cinema? There is a really funny film on."

"I don't feel like it," sighed Gabriella.

"Come on, you need to have a bit of fun, you work all hours, you need to let your hair down."

"I would prefer to just stay here and do something."

"Gabby it's not going to make a huge difference to your bank balance!" Maria joked sarcastically.

"I know; I just don't feel like going to the cinema."

"You really are serious about this travelling?" said Maria.

"You know I am."

"Well we have to do something? Let's meet the others down at the lakes."

"Okay."

The lakes were beautiful, especially in the summer. This was the local gathering place where they could swim and it was free! All of Gabriella's friends knew of her travelling plans, some of them would tease her about it, only because they were envious, the others were very excited for her.

"I wish I had your confidence to travel alone," exclaimed Angelica. "Are you not scared?"

"Not at all I'm excited, just one more year."

"Gabby! Angelica! Come on its lovely in here," shouted Maria.

It was an extremely hot day so the water was very inviting and refreshing.

"What are you going to wear for your party tomorrow," asked Maria?

"I'm not sure yet, something very glamorous!" laughed Gabriella.

And with that they enjoyed the rest of the day having fun at the lakes.

Next morning Gabriella woke up full of excitement, mama and papa were organising a party with family and friends for Gabriella's birthday. papa made a beautiful cake with lots of lovely different fruits, and mama made salads, pasta dishes and prepared different kinds of meat, and of course some yummy Rossini pastries. Gabriella loved family gatherings especially birthday ones!

"Morning Gabriella," smiled mama and papa. "Happy birthday Bella," they said, giving her a big hug. "Now, what would the birthday girl like for breakfast?"

"Ooh, pancakes and blueberries please with a glass of freshly squeezed orange."

So, what are you going to do today whilst we get prepared for your party?"

"I am going to meet my friends for a milkshake and just hang out."

"That sounds nice but please makes sure you are back in time to get ready for your party."

"I will," replied Gabriella as she went to get ready. "Thank you for the lovely breakfast." She kissed her mother goodbye.

Gabriella met her friends at café shake.

"Happy Birthday Gabby!" shouted her friends.

"Thanks everyone."

"So what did you get?" asked Marco.

"Don't be so rude," replied Angelica.

"What! I only asked what she got for her birthday, what's wrong with that?"

They all laughed.

"I don't know yet," beamed Gabriella, "I get them tonight."

"Well, we have all chipped in," smiled Angelica, "it's not a lot but we thought it could go towards you're travelling funds." She gave Gabriella 80 euro's.

"Guys, thank you so much, that will help a lot."

"Just one year to go," added Maria. "Have you planned where you want to go?"

"I have, I will tell you nearer the time. Let's enjoy today and look forward to tonight!"

***

"Gabriella, are you nearly ready? Your guests will be here soon."

"Yes I'm coming."

Gabriella wore a lovely sky blue halter neck dress that just passed her knees, white flat shoes and accessories. She felt very glamorous.

"Gabriella you look beautiful," beamed her proud parents.

"Thank you. I feel beautiful."

The guests started to arrive, wishing Gabriella a happy birthday.

"Grazie," she replied.

The Rossini's were a big family there were so many uncles, aunts, cousins. It took a while to greet everyone, and then all of Gabriella's friends started to arrive.

"You look great Gabby."

"Thank you, you all look great too."

"Wow there are so many people here," remarked Angelica.

"I know. My parents invite the whole family to everything!" she said smiling.

The evening was going really well. There was a lot to eat and drink, some of the uncles were entertaining everyone with music and songs, which got people up and dancing. Everyone was having a great time, especially Gabriella.

"Can I have your attention everyone," announced papa. "First, I would like to thank everyone for coming to celebrate our little bambino's birthday."

"Papa!" sighed an embarrassed Gabriella.

"Sorry, I mean our very grown up beautiful daughter." Everyone laughed. "And thank you all for your kind gifts. I would like you all to raise your glass to Gabriella."

"Now bring in the cake!"

It was a very big cake made with lots of lovely fresh fruit. It took two people to carry it. As the cake was being brought in Gabriella screamed. It was being carried by her brother Michael who had flown in especially from Paris. As he put the cake down Gabriella ran and threw her arms around him.

"What are you doing here?"

"I wouldn't have missed your birthday sis, plus mama and papa would never forgive me!"

They both laughed. Everyone clapped and cheered, there were tears as well, as the family came to hug Michael.

The evening continued for a few more hours then the guests started leaving. Gabriella said her goodbyes and thanked everyone for coming.

"See you tomorrow Gabby, thanks for a great night," said her friends, each giving her a big hug.

"Phew," yawned Gabriella as she flopped into the chair. "I'm exhausted."

"Did you have a good time Bella?"

"I had the best time."

The main family were still there, it was a Rossini tradition that all the children and their families stay for the opening of the presents. The first present was from her brother Anthony. It was Gabriella's favourite and very expensive perfume. Mario's gift was a store card to a designer clothes shop. A beautiful necklace from Michael and two hundred euro's from her parents, plus all the other presents from family and friends.

"Thank you all so much, I have had a wonderful evening I love you all."

Anthony, Mario and their families left. mama and papa started to clear away the mess.

"Leave that," said Michael, "Gabriella and I will do it. Go and rest."

"Grazie, we are quite tired." They kissed Gabriella and Michael goodnight.

"Why didn't you tell me you were coming home?"

"Well if I had told you then it wouldn't have been a surprise!" Michael exclaimed, playfully hitting her.

"I've missed you Michael, how long are you staying for?"

"Just a few days, I have to get back to work."

"How are things in Paris?"

"You would love it there Gabby, it's such a beautiful city, the people are great and the food is sooo good!"

"Don't let mama and papa hear you say that, there's nothing better than Italian food!" They both laughed. "So when do you think you will have your own restaurant?"

"Not for a while yet, I need to finish my training, then we will see what happens."

"Do you think you will come back?"

"I'm not sure; I do love it in Paris. I have a good part time job working in a top class restaurant, lots of friends. It would be hard to leave."

"Mama and papa will not be happy!" stated Gabriella.

"I know, but it's my life and I have to do what's right for me, just like you do!"

"They are going to go mad when I tell them I'm off travelling next year."

"Well I suggest you start telling them soon so they get used to it," encouraged Michael. "I can tell you all of the best places to visit when you go to Paris."

"I'm so glad you're home Michael, even if it is for only a few days."

The birthday celebrations came to an end and Michael had gone back to Paris. Gabriella started planning her travels. Even though it was still a year away, she wanted to get organised. Now for the hard part, how to tell her parents!

She started to leave brochures of different cities in Europe around the house, she left them in the kitchen, the lounge, even the bathroom, but mama would just tidy them away with everything else. Hmm that don't seem to be working she thought. I need to try something else. She phoned Maria.

"What can I do? They don't seem to be getting it."

"Why don't you just tell them," commented Maria.

"Are you mad!? They will go totally crazy; look how they were when Michael told them he was going to Paris to study to become a chef? I'll be going from one country to another by myself. No, it needs to be done in stages."

"Well good luck with that one," laughed Maria.

***

The year was passing by quickly, and the patisserie was as busy as ever. Gabriella was asked to tutor more students with their English which was great, lots more money towards her travels, but still she had not told her parents. "Right they have not got the hint so I guess I will have to tell them." But each time she went to say something Gabriella would chicken out! Come on Gabriella pull yourself together she said to herself, I'll do it tonight.

When the patisserie had closed for the day Gabriella made a cup of tea for her parents.

"Thank you Bella, it's good to sit down, it has been a long, busy day."

"Mama, papa I need to talk to you." Here goes, she thought.

"What's wrong Bella?"

"Well do you remember when I was little and I use to say that one day I wanted to travel around Europe?"

"Yes," laughed papa, "just a silly phase you went through."

Oh my god, this is harder than I thought, she said to herself. "Well I still feel like that. I've been saving my money since I can remember and now I have enough saved and I am going travelling next year once I turn twenty."

Her parents just looked at each other in silence. Gabriella sat there holding her breath waiting for their reaction, but nothing.

"I'm really tired," announced mama "think I'll go to bed."

"Me too," said papa, we have an early start in the morning."

"But it's still early!" blurted Gabriella.

"Goodnight Bella."

Gabriella sat there not quite sure what had just happened; maybe they need to sleep on it she thought.

When Gabriella got up the next morning her parents had already left for work. Now normally Gabriella would go with them, so the fact that they did not wait for her meant they were still upset.

Well they can't avoid me forever, she thought, I'll see them at the patisserie.

When Gabriella arrived at the patisserie it was like nothing had happened.

"Gabriella, customers need serving," said mama, not even looking at her.

I'll speak to them later, thought Gabriella.

It had been another busy day, mama and papa hardly said a word to Gabriella it was awful. They were all tired, mama cooked dinner and Gabriella washed up, and still her parents didn't speak to her.

"This is silly," Gabriella pointed out to her parents. "We need to talk about this."

"What are you talking about?" replied papa

"You know exactly what I'm talking about! I know you don't approve of me wanting to travel, but it is something I have always wanted to do, and I want to do it before I settle down, it will be a wonderful experience."

"It may be a wonderful experience for you whilst your mama and

I sit here day after day worrying about you, and if you are safe. You are a young women travelling alone. How do you expect us not to be concerned?"

"I understand that you are worried, but I will be fine."

"So where will you stay?"

"In hostels."

"Hostels!" papa shrieked throwing his hands in the air.

"Yes, it will be organised by a tour company, it is completely safe. There will be lots of other people going."

Mama started to cry.

"Look what you have done; you're breaking your mama's heart."

"I'm really sorry you're upset," acknowledged Gabriella "but I am going, and I would like to go with your blessing."

"Never," yelled papa.

Gabriella just looked at him and walked away.

***

Things were not very good at the Rossini's; Gabriella's parents would hardly speak to her. She went to see Maria.

"It went well then?" laughed Maria.

"Don't," huffed Gabriella, "it was awful. You would have thought I had committed some terrible crime!"

"Well in their eyes you have."

I'm nearly twenty, old enough to make my own choices."

"Gabby you are an only daughter of two very catholic, stuck in their way Italians, what do you expect, family is very important."

"I know what you're saying Maria but I expect them to be a bit more understanding."

"Give it time," advised Maria, "there's still six months, I'm sure they will come around?"

"I won't hold my breath!"

Gabriella's Travels by Jenny Ford, read more at:
www.theendlessbookcase.com/books/gabriellas-travels/

Printed in Great Britain
by Amazon

81523414R00119